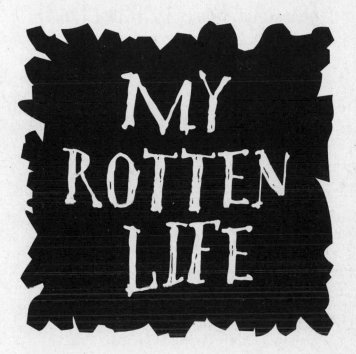

Starscape Books by David Lubar

NOVELS

Flip
Hidden Talents
True Talents

STORY COLLECTIONS

The Battle of the Red Hot Pepper Weenies,
And Other Warped and Creepy Tales

The Curse of the Campfire Weenies,
And Other Warped and Creepy Tales

In the Land of the Lawn Weenies,
And Other Warped and Creepy Tales

Invasion of the Road Weenies,
And Other Warped and Creepy Tales

Nathan Abercrombie, Accidental Zombie
BOOK 1

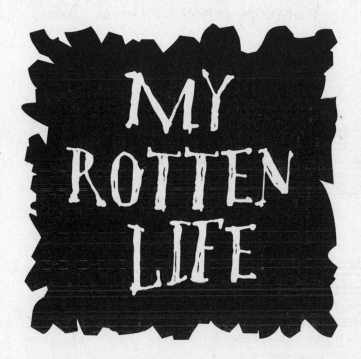

MY ROTTEN LIFE

David Lubar

A Tom Doherty Associates Book · New York

This is a work of fiction. All of the characters, organizations, and events portrayed in this novel are either products of the author's imagination or are used fictitiously.

MY ROTTEN LIFE

Copyright © 2009 by David Lubar

Reading Group Guide © 2009 by Tor Books

All rights reserved.

A Starscape Book
Published by Tom Doherty Associates, LLC
175 Fifth Avenue
New York, NY 10010

www.tor-forge.com

Library of Congress Cataloging-in-Publication Data

Lubar, David.
  My rotten life / David Lubar.—1st ed.
     p. cm.
  "A Tom Doherty Associates Book."
  Summary: Tired of continually having his feelings hurt by popular students and bullies, fifth-grader Nathan agrees to try an experimental formula, Hurt-Be-Gone, and becomes a half-dead zombie which has, he soon discovers, some real advantages.
  ISBN: 978-0-7653-2508-2 (hc)
  ISBN: 978-0-7653-1634-9 (pbk)
  [1. Self-confidence—Fiction. 2. Popularity—Fiction. 3. Schools—Fiction. 4. Zombics—Fiction. 5. Experiments—Fiction.] I. Title.
  PZ7.L96775My 2009
  [Fic]—dc22

                                                        2008035762

First Edition: August 2009

Printed in January 2010 in the United States of America by
RR Donnelley, Harrisonburg, Virginia

0   9   8   7   6   5   4

For Joelle and Alison,
who make life good

CONTENTS

▼

INTRODUCTION

▼

My best friend and I used to have contests where we'd try to gross each other out. We don't bother with that anymore. I can win every time, even when I'm not trying.

Ouch

It's no fun having your heart ripped from your body, slammed to the floor, and stomped into a puddle of quivering red mush. It's even less fun when it happens three times in one afternoon.

First, Shawna Lanchester pranced up to me at lunch and said, "Did you know I'm having a Halloween party next Friday, Nathan?" She clutched her hands together like she was in danger of exploding from excitement.

I nodded, but I kept my mouth shut. I really didn't want to risk spraying Shawna with ketchup-coated hamburger particles. Girls are really weird about food once it's been chewed even a little bit. Especially girls who dress like they're about to pose for a magazine cover.

I knew about the party. The whole planet knew. Or, at least, the whole fifth grade. Shawna had a big Halloween party every year. I'd never been invited. Nobody at our table had ever been invited. I'd bet nobody at our table had ever talked with Shawna, either, even though we'd been in school together since kindergarten. I was making all sorts of history.

Shawna bounced on her heels. Her light-brown hair danced off her tanned shoulders. "Guess what?"

"Mmmmwwwtt?" That's how *what* sounds if you keep your lips pressed together when you talk. I tore my dull brown eyes away from Shawna's dazzling green ones just long enough to prove to myself what I'd suspected. Everyone was watching me. Mookie, Adam, Denali, and the other Second Besters at our pathetic table under the leak in the cafeteria ceiling were all staring at me like I'd just won the lottery, or the Super Bowl.

To my right, at least half the nerds had looked up from their chessboards, handheld games, and dungeon maps. To my left, the kids stuck at the Table of the Doomed were watching. Snail Girl—I didn't even know her real name—was staring at me over the top of her Sammy the Snail lunch box. As always, she was dressed in one of her endless snail shirts and wearing snail hair clips. Ferdinand Zweeler flinched when I caught his eye. Ferdinand was so frightened of everything, he should have been named Feardinand. Even weird Abigail, who came here last year from outer space—and still seems to live in deep space—had turned her head halfway in my direction.

The jocks, the skaters, and everyone else at all the large rectangular tables in the cafeteria were watching. I struggled to keep from grinning in triumph. Finally, the girl I'd had a crush on since third grade had noticed me. I wondered whether it was my new spiky haircut. Or the fact that I'd grown two inches over the summer. I snuck another glance at Mookie—the only person on the planet who knew how I felt. He flashed me a thumbs-up.

Shawna smiled. My heart melted.

Her teeth glistened. Her eyes sparkled. Her lips moved.

"You're not invited."

Rip. Slam. Stomp.

My heart splatted to the floor. It lay there, leaking across the tiles like a dropped scoop of raspberry sherbet.

Shawna spun away, grinding the remains of my heart under her heels. I tried to ignore the giggles that burst from Cydnie, Talissa, Bekkah, Lexi, and the other girls at her table, but I had a hard time swallowing.

I risked a quick glance around the cafeteria. The nerds had already gone back to slaying orcs and capturing castles. The jocks had gone back to punching one another. The Doomed were still staring. I guess it was a rare treat for them to see someone else get destroyed.

"Wow, that's totally cruel." Mookie pushed his glasses back up his nose, trapping some of the longer strands of his shaggy hair under the thick plastic frame. "I wonder why she picked you?"

I choked down the rest of my overchewed mouthful as I searched for an answer. "No idea. You'd think it would be enough for her to be popular, without having to crush the rest of us." I wanted to reach for my inhaler, but there was no way I was pulling it out right now.

"Popularity is overrated," Mookie said. "You don't have to be popular to have lots of friends."

Nobody bothered to answer him. We all knew the truth—in fifth grade, popularity was everything. As far as I could tell, part of popularity came from who you were, and part came from what you could do. Either way, the eight of us at the Second Besters table would score somewhere around minus two on a popularity scale of one to ten.

We were all second best—or maybe second worst—in some way. Mookie Vetch was the second-fattest kid in the fifth grade. I was the second-skinniest boy. Adam Kessler was the second-smartest kid, Denali Sherborg was the second-funniest girl, Jenny Chung was the second-best singer, Jerome Tully was the second-messiest kid, and Armando Cadiz was a triple-threat second bester who was the second-best dresser, the second-worst chatterbox, and the second-fastest reader in class.

The fattest kid, the skinniest boy, the funniest girl—they all had some kind of recognition that made them visible. Being second didn't mean anything. I guess it was sort of like being vice president. To tell the truth, Mookie wasn't all that fat, and I wasn't all that skinny. We pretty much weren't all that much of anything, except unnoticed.

"Typical bullying behavior," Adam said. "She's putting you down so she can feel better about herself."

"Thanks." I already knew that. Every kid who'd ever been picked on knew that. Our parents told us that. Our teachers told us that. Cute animated reptiles and vegetables on television told us that. It didn't help.

"I guess right now, she feels totally great about herself," Denali said.

The rest of the table laughed. I smiled, but it wasn't real.

When the bell rang, Mookie and I headed for gym. We had it three times a week, together with the boys from Mr. Walpole's home base. I'm not sure who decided it would be a great idea for kids to load up on grease-coated meat and deep-fried starch, topped off with a huge bowl of butterscotch pudding, and then do sit-ups. If I ever run into that genius, he's going to get kicked real hard in the stomach. Not that violence solves anything.

"Move it!" Mr. Lomux screamed as our class shuffled

out the gym door toward the track. "We can't afford to waste time." Blue veins, like tiny candy worms, bulged on his shaved head.

"Seven?" I asked Mookie.

He squinted and started counting on his fingers. "I see eight."

"Oh, man—that's bad." We could always tell how angry Mr. Lomux was by counting veins. "I've never seen more than six." That was way back in third grade, when he'd made us do too many jumping jacks during a heat wave and half the class puked on the gym floor.

"I think he's stressed about field day," Mookie said.

"I heard that the school board is threatening to transfer him to the lower elementary school if he loses again." Our school, Belgosi Upper Elementary, had a big competition each year against Perrin Hall Academy in Hurston Lakes. The entire fifth grade of each school competed. They'd beaten us six times in a row. Hurston Lakes whomps our butts at everything. They have three elementary schools and at least five private schools.

East Craven is one of the smallest towns in New Jersey. All we have is Belgosi Upper and Borloff Lower. People keep moving out of town. Dad said it's all because of money. People who have a lot move to Hurston Lakes. People who want to spend less move across the river to Pennsylvania. Either way, people are leaving.

Ours is the smallest fifth grade ever, with 144 kids in six classes.

"I need four captains," Mr. Lomux said. "We're going to break up into teams to practice."

A bunch of hands shot up.

"Pick me! Pick me!" Mookie screamed, waving his arms like he was trying to flag down an airplane.

A ninth vein appeared.

I didn't bother raising my hand. We're all supposed to get a chance to be a captain. But Mr. Lomux mostly picks the same sort of kids over and over. Today he picked Mort Ivanson, who's really fast; Rodney Mullasco, who's really big; and the Decker twins, who are the stars of the basketball team.

The four of them studied us like shoppers searching for the best melon in the supermarket. As their eyes flickered past me, I realized there was something much worse than not getting to be a captain.

I imagined myself standing alone on the edge of the field, watching everyone else join a team. *Don't let me be picked last.* Not today, when I was still waiting for my heart to crawl from the cafeteria floor and back through the gaping hole in my chest.

I tried to catch Mort's eye. He was the nicest of the four, and the only one I'd ever hung out with—even though it was way back in second grade. He looked at me and smiled. This was great. Maybe I'd be picked first for a change. That would help save this from being a to-tally rotten day.

The captains began making their picks. Mort pointed at me. I started to trot over to join him. Things were fi-nally going my way.

2

The Last Gasp

"I **got Daniel**," Mort said, picking the kid right next to me.

I froze in midstep, then shuffled back into the mob, hoping nobody had noticed.

The other captains took their picks.

"Lance."

"I'll take Mick."

"Come on, Trevor."

All the fastest and strongest kids got picked first, leaving the average and the weak huddled on the field.

"Me, me, me!" Mookie kept screaming.

I guess it worked. He got picked right after all the

kids who were actually good at sports. He's hefty, but he's fast on his feet, even though he tends to fall.

I'm not the greatest athlete in the world. I didn't play a lot of sports when I was little, so I don't have as much experience as the other kids. But I knew I was better than Dilby "The Digger" Parkland or Ferdinand. Dilby goes through life off balance because he usually keeps one hand jammed in his nose, his ear, his armpit, or other places I don't even want to know about, and Ferdinand ran like he was wearing glass sneakers.

Soon, there were only five of us left. Me, Dilby, Ferdinand, and two kids who sat with Ferdinand at the Table of the Doomed. For once, I wouldn't have minded being second, or even third. But after Rodney picked Dilby, and Mort picked Ferdinand, my face started to flush.

One of the Doomed got snagged. I could hear my pulse pounding on both sides of my head. I started to wish I'd used my inhaler in the cafeteria. In my mind, I was jumping and screaming like Mookie. *Pick me! Pick me!*

Several terrible seconds later, I was alone on the field. Last pick. Actually, I guess I wasn't even a pick. I was a remainder—like yesterday's unfinished green bean casserole. I wanted to joke about it—Hey, *saving the best for last*—but I felt like someone had duct-taped my lungs to my ribs.

"Teammate!" Dilby pulled his hand from his armpit and offered me a high five as I walked over to join Rodney's team. I swear I could almost see fumes rising from Dilby's fingers, rippling the air. I waved at him, then put my hands behind my back. No way I wanted to slap that diseased palm of his.

"Loser." Rodney punched my shoulder. "Don't mess us up." He was such a bully, I figured he was the first-, second-, and third-meanest kid in class. If we were suddenly transformed into animals, Rodney would be a combination of a gorilla and a slug. He already had a greasy head and dangerous eyes. I was really glad I only had to see him at gym, recess, and lunch.

He gave me another punch. "And keep away from Shawna."

Oh, great. He must have seen her talking to me at lunch, and not realized she was only there to slice off large hunks of my flesh for the amusement of her friends. Everybody knew Rodney had a big-time crush on Shawna. That's one of the many reasons I kept my own crush a secret from everyone except for Mookie. But Shawna liked athletes, not killers, so Rodney hadn't gotten anywhere.

"Sure," I said. "I promise I'll stay away from her." Yeah, that wouldn't be a hard promise to keep.

We started with the mile run. I hated it. I was okay for the first half, but then I always ran out of air. Mom wanted me to get a note from the doctor excusing me from gym, but there was no way I was going to do that.

The girls were running, too, which made it even worse.

They started after we'd already run two laps, which meant they were still fresh while we were getting tired. Most of them passed me. Even Abigail. Mort lapped me twice. I came in last, gasping and wheezing.

"Abercrombie!" Mr. Lomux yelled. "I've seen babies crawl faster than you run."

I looked past him at the girls, who'd gathered around their gym teacher, Ms. Gristle. They didn't pay any attention to us. Everyone was used to Mr. Lomux shouting. But that didn't make it hurt any less. I knew they'd heard him.

It's not like I wanted to be a bad runner. I was born three or four weeks earlier than I was supposed to, and my lungs aren't super great. I guess I have asthma, though I don't like to call it that, because I'm not really sick or anything. It's not a problem, except when I'm running. Or if I get really upset.

I managed to survive the high jump and the broad jump without hurting myself. Then I went to the crossbar for chin-ups. I did okay there, since I didn't have a lot of weight to lift. But nobody ever got popular because he was good at something as unimportant as chin-ups.

"Gather up!" Mr. Lomux shouted right before the end of the period. He glanced down at his clipboard. "Good job, Ivanson. You, too, Blakely." He praised a couple more kids, then turned toward me. "Abercrombie, Zweeler, Parkland, you're killing us. If you don't improve,

22

you're taking the whole school down with you. Is that what you want?"

Great. No pressure there.

"We need this win," he said. "We have to get this win. And when we do, I'm treating the whole fifth grade to a pizza party."

Most of the kids cheered. But the cheers faded as reality sank in. Nobody expected us to win.

"Better tie those," I told Mookie when we were leaving the field. His laces flopped from his sneakers like baby snakes chasing after two white rats. He'd pulled them loose as soon as gym was finished.

"It's cooler this way," he said.

"You're going to trip."

"I trip anyhow. So I might as well be cool."

"Just don't fall on me." We headed back to home base for reading with Mrs. Otranto. Mookie only fell on me twice, which was pretty good for him.

Mrs. Otranto let us read for the whole period, so the only danger I faced was a paper cut. I got to spend forty-five minutes reading about someone whose life was far worse than mine. That was sort of nice. Finally, it was time for my last class of the day.

"I'll see you after specials," I told Mookie.

"You're lucky you got art this marking period," he said as he dug his drumsticks out of his desk. "I thought music would be fun."

"It's nowhere near as good as it is in the video games," Adam said as he dragged his tuba case from the coat closet.

"Few things are." I headed for the art room, along with Denali. I had to hustle to keep up with her. She was always eager to get to art, but not for the normal reason. Her enthusiasm had nothing to do with drawing or painting.

"Maybe this will be the day," I said.

"Maybe," she said. "I'm feeling lucky."

As usual, Mr. Dorian was the last person to get to the room. He was big-time hooked on coffee, and always ducked out to the teachers' lounge between classes to refill his mug.

When he came in, he said, "Take out your sketch pads. We're going to continue to work on perspective today." He slipped his gray smock over his head. He always wore it, even though I'd never seen him paint or draw. He just sat in his chair and drank coffee.

We'd been drawing for about five minutes when Mr. Dorian said, "Don't forget what I showed you about foreshortening."

He lifted his coffee cup and took a sip. That's when Denali sprang. "Hey, since this is fifth grade, shouldn't we use fiveshortening?"

I didn't think it was all that great a joke, but Denali's timing was perfect. Mr. Dorian laughed before he had a chance to swallow. Coffee sprayed from his nose. He dropped the cup, spilling the rest in his lap. I guess it wasn't very hot, because he didn't scream. But he leaped from his chair and stared down at his soaked legs.

I gave Denali a thumbs-up. "Score."

"My life is complete," she said.

Mr. Dorian headed for the hallway. "I'll be right back. Keep working. No fooling around."

The instant the door closed behind him, nearly every kid in the room whipped out a PSP, DS, or other portable game. Nearly everyone except for Abigail, who was staring at the table, and me. I didn't have one. Mom thought games were too violent. Dad thought they were a bad investment.

I looked over to my left and watched Caleb Harris play a game. It was pretty cool. He was running around, shooting zombies. Okay, I'll admit it was violent. But it wasn't like he was shooting real people or anything.

I laughed as Caleb's guy got sliced in half with a chain saw. "I didn't know zombies could use power tools," I said.

He glared at me. "Be quiet. This is hard."

"Sorry." It didn't look that hard.

"Phooey," he said a moment later, stomping his foot. "I lost again."

"Can I try?" I was dying to play something good. I got to play games at Mookie's house, but all he had was this extremely ancient Nintendo.

"It's really hard," Caleb said.

"That's okay. I'm pretty good," I lied.

"Here, I'll set it on easy." He went to the menu screen. "You start with ten guys."

"You don't have to do that. I can handle it."

Caleb just smirked and passed me the game.

I hit START. Three seconds later, I was dead. Zombies swarmed my corpse and fought over my brain. I lost my next guy four seconds after that. As I tried to avoid the waves of zombies with my third man, I heard Caleb say, "Hey, Nathan's setting a record on *Zombie Invasion*. Check it out!"

I felt people crowding around behind me, leaning over my shoulder. I wanted to give the game back to Caleb, but I couldn't quit with everyone watching. And I knew I could do better.

As I lost my next guy, someone said, "What record?"

"A record for fastest loser," Caleb said.

I glanced at him and lost another guy. Everyone was leaning over me. I felt like they were stealing all the air in the room. I couldn't get past the first mob of zombies. Every time I even blinked, I lost another man.

"Loser," someone said.

"Idiot."

"You mean vidiot," someone else said.

"Yeah, Nathan's a vidiot."

"Can't play games."

"Can't even play easy games."

"Total vidiot loser."

I was down to my last man. The buttons grew slippery under my damp thumbs. I wanted to put down the game and run from the room. I couldn't even do that. The mob surrounded me, just like the mindless zombies in the game. Except, instead of eating my brain, they were stomping my heart.

The door slammed. "You call this working?"

Everyone scrambled back to their seats as Mr. Dorian stormed over to me. "Nathan, I'm surprised at you." He snatched the game from my hands and said, "You can have this back at the end of the period."

"Vidiot," someone whispered.

I held out as long as I could, hoping nobody would pay any more attention to me. Then I pulled out my inhaler. The hiss echoed through the room like a grenade blast.

I waited for the period to end and tried not to think about anything. My mind had other ideas—it forced me to think about everything.

Not invited.

Last pick.

Total vidiot loser.

I stayed at the table after everyone else left, even though I knew Mookie was waiting for me. The afternoon swirled through my mind. I could pretend to laugh and joke about the smackdowns. But they hurt. They hurt a lot. If someone stabbed my tongue with a mustard-coated screwdriver, it wouldn't have hurt this much.

I was so totally crushed that I really didn't care what else happened to me. I figured there was no way things could get any worse.

Boy, was I wrong.

3

Life Science

"**Hey, Nate. Come** on, school's over. What's wrong? Did you sit on glue?"

"I wish. At least then, all I'd have to do is slip out of my pants and walk home in my underwear. That, I could handle."

Mookie plopped down on the corner of the table. "Whoa. You sound totally bummed. You aren't still upset about Shawna, are you?"

"That's a couple layers down." I described part three of my perfect day.

"Who cares what they think?" Mookie said. "Let's get out of here."

Mookie followed me as I slumped through the hall and down the front steps.

"Yaaahhhh!"

I spun at the sound of his scream and managed to catch him as he tripped.

"Hey, thanks. You saved my life."

"Whatever." I wasn't feeling heroic. I was barely feeling human.

"Cheer up. None of this stuff is important."

I didn't bother to answer him. He hadn't lived through any of my three-part nightmare, except as a witness.

"It really doesn't matter," he said. "It's just school."

"That's not true! It matters." I smacked a tree with my palm. That was a mistake, but I was too angry to care about the pain. "Just school? We pretty much spend our whole lives in school. So if school stinks, then life stinks."

"I know." He dropped his backpack to the ground and leaned against the tree. "It was a total lie. I wanted to make you feel better. And lying is usually a pretty good way to cheer people up. My parents always lie to me when I'm sad. Nobody wants to hear the truth."

"Thanks for trying."

"Did it work?" he asked.

"Absolutely," I said. "I feel a whole lot better."

"Are you lying?"

"Of course I'm lying. I don't think anything is going

to make me feel better. I just wish I didn't spend so much time feeling bad. You know what—I wish I didn't have any feelings at all."

I heard a quiet voice from behind me. "I can help."

I spun around. It was Abigail. I don't think I'd ever heard her talk before. She never raised her hand in class. She sat in the back and seemed to be lost in her own little world. When she'd first moved here, there'd been all sorts of rumors about her family. Denali said they were in the witness protection program, and Adam swore they were traveling gypsies. But nothing weird or exciting ever happened around her, so everyone pretty much lost interest. Now she was telling me she could help.

"What are you talking about?"

She reached in her backpack and pulled out a candy bar. "Before I tell you, have some chocolate. It's not a cure, but it will make you feel a little bit better."

"No thanks." I really didn't want to take candy from strange girls. "I'm not in the mood for chocolate."

"I am!" Mookie snatched the bar from her hand, tore it open, and crammed the whole thing in his mouth. "You're right. I feel great now. And sorta jumpy." Wet, brown bubbles formed at his lips as he spoke.

"I was offering to share." Abigail stared at him for a moment, then turned back to me. "I saw what happened to you today. You must be hurting. I really do know something that can help, way more than chocolate."

31

"Like what?" I wondered whether she was going to ask me to join some weird club or sing a happy song. I wasn't even close.

"My uncle Zardo is a neurobiologist," she said. "He's studying emotions. He's developing some sort of secret formula to get rid of unwanted feelings, and he needs to start testing it."

"That sounds dangerous," Mookie said.

"He's totally brilliant," Abigail said. "If anybody can help you, it would be him. Let's go to his lab. He works across town at RCC."

"Whatever kind of joke this is, play it on someone else," I said. "I've had enough for one day."

"That's the reason why you should come," Abigail said. "Because you've had such a bad day. Trust me. Do I look like someone who plays tricks on people?"

She had a point. She definitely looked more like a victim than like a bully. She was short, with frizzy brown hair and freckles. She had big puppy eyes and the smile of a five-year-old. As I tried to decide what to do, Shawna and her two best friends walked past. Shawna didn't look at me, but Cydnie and Lexi pointed in my direction and giggled.

I reached in my pocket, wrapped my fingers around my inhaler, and rested my thumb against the top of the canister.

Not invited.

Picked last.

Total vidiot loser.

The world had already done its best to take my breath away. I really didn't have much left to lose. "Let's go."

"Bad idea," Mookie said. "Science is dangerous. I've seen too many movies where people turn into insects because of science. You want to end up with six legs and a stinger?"

I didn't bother to answer that question. "Are you coming or not?"

He grabbed his backpack. "Sure. It's not like I have anything else to do. Besides, I guess it would be cool to see you turn into an insect. You could fly us all over the place. Hey—if you became a mosquito, you could drain Shawna's blood. Though it might give you brain freeze."

We crossed Belgosi Road, then turned down Davis Street toward Romero Community College, which was right past the center of town, near the park.

"Why are you helping me?" I asked Abigail.

"Because you smiled at me."

"Huh? When?"

"Last year. My third day in school. It was the Wednesday before Thanksgiving vacation. You were the first person to smile at me. The only one, actually."

Normally, there was no way I'd remember that sort of thing. But that was the morning Mom told me she'd gotten us tickets for the circus. I'd smiled at everyone that day. Even Mr. Lomux. But I wasn't going to admit it to

33

Abigail, so I changed the subject. "It must be tough moving to a new school."

"There are harder things to deal with," she said.

"Like cafeteria pizza," Mookie said.

"And like . . ." Abigail stopped, as if she didn't want to say any more.

"Like what?" I asked.

"Nothing." She turned away from me and pushed the button at the light across the street from the college.

It was weird going onto a college campus. Everyone looked a lot more serious than they did in our school, and a lot taller. But nobody seemed to mind that we were there. The students didn't even glance at us. I guess once you're in college, you're almost an adult—which means you pay no attention to kids.

Abigail led us into the Moreau Science Building, and up two flights of stairs to a door marked RESEARCH LAB.

The lab looked sort of like the science room in school, except it had more equipment, fewer tables, and no safety posters. I'd bet there wasn't any gum stuck under the stools, either. A man in a white lab coat stood at a workbench, mixing some powders together and humming "Deck the Halls." He was off-key and off season. His slicked-back hair made his bushy black eyebrows stand out like fuzzy caterpillars.

"Hello, Twinkle," he said when we walked in.

"Twinkle?" I whispered to Mookie.

Abigail shot me a glare and whispered, "I will kill you

34

if you ever utter that word again." She turned to her uncle. "I brought someone to meet you. Nathan is tired of getting his feelings hurt. He's a perfect test subject."

I expected Abigail's uncle to toss me one of those stupid adult sayings like "It will get better," or "Don't pay any attention to mean people. They just envy you."

Instead, he looked around like he was making sure nobody could hear us. Then he rushed over and closed the door. The whole time, he rubbed his hands together like he was about to dive into a Thanksgiving feast.

I glanced at Mookie and then at the door, wondering whether we should leave. I decided to get some more information first. "What, exactly, do you do?" I asked.

"I'm working on isolating the biochemical source of emotions," he said. "I believe I've discovered a safe way to neutralize bad feelings."

"How?" I noticed that Abigail had gone over to one of the tables and started playing around with some sort of instrument that was spinning a bunch of test tubes.

"It's sort of complicated," he said.

"I'm not stupid," I told him. I'd gotten a B-minus on my last science test, which was pretty good since nobody can understand Ms. Delambre when she gets going at full speed."

"Well, I'm using protease-based inhibitors to attempt to invert the action of kinase enhancers, effectively targeting the nucleus of the dendrite. . . ."

He said another hundred or so words, but I lost track

somewhere between *protease* and *dendrite*. Or it might have been at *Well*. I glanced at Mookie again, but he was busy shaking hands with a skeleton that was shoved in one corner of the lab.

"Definitely the skinniest guy in the room," Mookie said.

Abigail, who was still messing around with the equipment, acted like she was listening. I figured she didn't have a clue, either.

Her uncle pulled a key from his lab coat, unlocked a metal cabinet, then opened the cabinet door. There was a safe inside the cabinet. He turned the dial, opened the safe, and dragged out a large glass jar filled with a purple liquid.

"Kool-Aid!" Mookie said. "Yay! I'll get some cups." He started digging around in a cabinet under the sink.

"Hardly," Abigail's uncle said as he unscrewed the lid. "This is Hurt-Be-Gone, the world's first all-natural, totally safe emotion killer. It takes only one tiny drop to wash away all your sorrows. We can even target specific hurts, or protect people from new ones. I'm going to be so rich. Finally."

"Found some!" Mookie waved a stack of plastic cups. "Let me pour. I love to pour." He dashed toward Abigail's uncle. Halfway there, he tripped on his own lace.

"Look out!" I yelled.

Mookie crashed into Abigail's uncle, knocking him

toward me. The jar went flying. I felt like I'd been smacked with an ocean wave.

My whole shirt was soaked with Hurt-Be-Gone. The stuff dripped down my face. It streamed down my arms and ran off my fingertips. I spat as I realized there was some in my mouth. I expected it to taste awful, but it didn't have any flavor at all.

Abigail's uncle stared at me like I'd just been sliced in half— the long way. "Uh-oh."

Abigail stared at me like I'd just been sliced in quarters. "Oh no." Her face turned so pale, her freckles looked like measles.

"What's wrong?"

"Nothing," Abigail's uncle said. "You'll be fine. Don't give it another thought." He grabbed a handful of paper towels and held them out to me like he was afraid to get too close.

"I ung's umb," I said as I took the towels.

"What?" he asked.

I tried again, speaking as carefully as I could. "My tongue's numb."

"Don't worry. I'm pretty sure that's not a problem. You'll be fine."

"Pretty sure?" I asked. "You're supposed to know this stuff."

Before he could answer, the door banged open and a stream of blue uniforms flooded the room. It looked like half the cops in East Craven were spilling into the lab.

"I didn't do it!" Mookie screamed. He threw his hands in the air and backed against a counter.

"Zardo Goldberg?" the cop in front asked, ignoring Mookie.

"Never heard of him," Abigail's uncle said.

Abigail raced to the window and flung it open. "Run, Uncle Zardo!" Then she glanced out, got even paler, slammed the window, and yelled, "Third floor. Forget it."

The cop looked down at a picture in his hand, and then back up at Abigail's uncle. "Zardo Goldberg, you're under arrest for the importation of endangered plant specimens without a license."

"But I need them for my research!" he shouted. "I'm on the verge of a breakthrough! It's for the good of all mankind."

The cops didn't seem to care about his research, or his breakthrough. They slapped on the cuffs and dragged him off. He kicked, thrashed, and begged like a hyperactive two-year-old being taken to his room for a nap. I guess he really didn't want to leave the lab.

Mookie and I stood there with our mouths hanging open.

Abigail sighed, pulled out a cell phone, pressed a button, and said, "Mom, Uncle Zardo is going to need bail again. Yeah, I'll be home soon. Love you, too. Bye."

"Again?" I asked.

Abigail shrugged. "He's had a colorful past."

While I was trying to figure out what that meant, Mookie said, "I wonder if it worked."

"Huh?" I didn't know what he was talking about.

"The Hurt-Be-Gone—do you think it got rid of your feelings? I mean, if a dose is one drop, you really got dosed big-time. Nothing should hurt your feelings. Not even a thousand Shawnas."

Just the mention of her name made my chest feel tight. "I don't think it worked."

Abigail poked me in the shoulder. "Your breath stinks, your nose is too big, and everybody hates you."

"Hey!" I shouted.

Abigail gave me an innocent smile. "Guess not."

"Yeah, it looks like it didn't work. I still have feelings." I held my hand up to my mouth, blew on it, and tried to smell my breath. It seemed fine to me. "You didn't really mean it about my breath, did you?"

"Of course not," Abigail said. She gazed up at me with those puppy-dog eyes. I wasn't sure whether to believe her.

"Aren't you worried about your uncle?" Mookie asked.

"Nah," Abigail said. "He gets arrested all the time. I think this is his third time for the year. He's kind of crazy."

"Crazy? And you brought me to his lab?"

"Hey, no harm," Abigail said. "Nothing bad happened. At least, not to you."

Boy, was *she* wrong.

Hurt Feelings

So," **Abigail asked** as we headed out of the lab, "what do you want to do?"

"Go home and take a shower." Whatever Uncle Crazy had spilled on me hadn't smelled bad at first. But now it smelled sort of like wet dirt mixed with really old cheese and cheap perfume. Definitely worse than Mookie's breath that time he ate a whole envelope of dry onion-soup mix, but not even close to the boy's locker room during wrestling season.

Mookie sniffed the air. "Better take two. And a bath."

"We could do something after that," Abigail said. "I know this great hiking trail in Ackerman's Woods."

Mookie shrugged like he didn't care either way. I wasn't really in the mood to hang out with Abigail. It was nice that she wanted to help me, but all she'd done was get me soaked with chemicals.

"I have homework and stuff," I said.

"Oh . . . okay." She reached in her bag and pulled out a piece of notepaper with her address and phone number printed at the top. "Here. Give me a call if anything unusual happens."

"Huh? Like what?"

"I don't know," Abigail said. "But Uncle Zardo would probably want to keep track of any effects. So keep in touch, okay?"

"Sure." I took the paper and walked off with Mookie.

"I like her," he said after we'd gone outside and crossed the street. "She sort of makes me seem normal."

"Almost," I said.

A block from home, my shirt fell to pieces. I stared at the shreds of cloth scattered on the ground at my feet.

"This isn't good," Mookie said. "Are you sure you're all right?"

I looked at my chest. My skin seemed okay. It tingled a little, but I figured that was from the cool air. "It's no big deal. I'm fine."

"Maybe you should call Abigail?"

"What's the point? She can't do anything for me." I just wanted to go home and forget about the whole day.

"Remember," Mookie said when we reached my house. "Two showers and a bath."

My folks were at work, so I didn't have to explain why I came home without a shirt. Mom works in a store that sells teddy bears. It's called Stuffy Wuffy. Really. She helps people find the perfect bear. Dad is an accountant. That means he helps people with their taxes.

After my shower, I went to my room and put on clean clothes, then took out my homework. I managed to finish before my folks got home. They both popped their heads into my room to say hi, ask how my day was, and then nod and smile when I told them my day was just fine. I really couldn't tell either of them how bad it was. Dad would just say, "Take it like a man." Mom would get all upset and call the principal. She sort of tries to protect me too much. That's why I didn't play any sports when I was little.

I was pretty tired by then. My tongue was still numb, and the skin on my chest felt even more tingly than before—like my upper body was falling asleep.

I was so wiped out, I spent most of the weekend in my room. I didn't even do anything with Mookie on Saturday. I slept so much that Mom kept asking me if I was feeling okay.

The sleep didn't seem to help. By Sunday evening, I felt like I was walking through a dream. My folks were cooking dinner when I came down to the kitchen. Dad was in charge of the salad, because that's the only thing he can make without poisoning anyone. Mom was frying burgers, because she isn't all that much better a cook than Dad, and it's pretty hard to ruin a burger, as long as you don't care how burned or raw it is. Besides, you can make almost anything taste good if you pile on enough pickles and ketchup.

Mom went to get the dishes from the cabinet. "Can you put the burgers on the table?" she asked.

"What?" I heard the words, but they didn't make much sense. My brain was totally fuzzy.

She pointed to the oven and spoke again. I forced myself to pay attention.

"Put the burgers on the table."

"Sure." I opened the oven door. Mom can never get the cheese to melt on the stove top, so she always finishes the burgers in the oven. As I grabbed the handle of the frying pan and turned toward the table, a scream ripped the air.

"Hot!!!!!" Mom yelled, racing toward me. "Hot! Hot! Hot! Drop it!"

I looked at my hand. Then I looked at the pot holder on the counter next to the oven. Then I looked back at my hand.

I dropped the pan, screamed, and braced myself for the wave of pain. I'd burned myself last summer when Dad was teaching me how to use a soldering iron, so I knew how badly burns could hurt. But the pain seemed to be taking a long time to get from my fingers to my brain.

Mom was making those weird whimpering noises that you can spell with nothing but vowels. She grabbed the sprayer from the sink and sprayed my hand with cold water. "Are you burned?"

I looked at my palm. It was a little red, but there weren't any blisters or anything. "No. I'm okay." I guess the pan wasn't that hot after all. My hand felt fine. The burgers, however, weren't doing too well. They'd bounced out of the pan and slid across the floor like greasy hockey pucks.

"Thank goodness you aren't hurt." Mom squeezed me in a hug. "You gave me such a scare. Don't ever do that again."

Dad grabbed the phone and hit number 2 on the speed dial. "I'll call for a pizza." He sounded relieved.

While we waited for dinner, I kept glancing at my hand. I couldn't believe it wasn't even the tiniest bit sore. After my horrible heart-stomping last Friday, I'd finally caught a lucky break. I guess I should have figured everything out right then. Maybe I would have if my brain wasn't so fuzzy.

But the truth was about to hit me right in the face.

5

I'll Take a Stab at That

Don't worry," Mookie said. "She's done with you."

"You think?" We were back at lunch. It was Monday. My tongue was still a little numb, but my brain was less fuzzy. I'd slept so well, Mom needed to wake me three times before I got out of bed. I kept glancing over at Shawna's table, wondering whether she was going to stomp on any of my other organs. Maybe she could put a kidney under each foot and do a tap routine, or rip out my lungs and use them as leg warmers.

"She's like a cat, and you're like a dead mouse. All the fun is gone. She's going to go after the next unsuspecting rodent." Mookie wrinkled his nose and sniffed like a mouse.

"Thanks. I feel a lot better knowing that." One table away from Shawna, Rodney was also staring at her, and talking loudly to his friends. I guess he was trying to impress her.

"Speaking of mice, I should have gotten the burger. It might be gray and dead, but it's soft." Mookie sawed away at his pizza brick.

That's what we call the rock-hard cafeteria pizza. You can't really bite it, unless you want to end up with a smile like a professional hockey player. Most of us just hack away with a knife and fork, trying to chip off small pieces. The sound of sawing could be heard all around the cafeteria. Mookie had somehow managed to eat half his pizza brick already.

I sawed at my own pizza. It was especially tough today. I guess the lunch ladies got an extra shipment of cement. I kept sawing, putting all my weight into it. My knife didn't even make a dent. I jabbed the pizza with my fork. It bounced off my tray and hit the table between me and Mookie. I didn't care—I wasn't really all that hungry.

"Die!" Mookie shouted, stabbing at my pizza with his fork.

The pizza flipped into the air and bounced back toward me.

"Death to the brick!" I shouted. I stabbed at it again.

It did a double flip with a half twist and landed on Mookie's tray.

"Acrobatic pizza! Awesome!" He grabbed his fork with both hands and slashed down at the pizza.

"Pizza hockey!" Denali shouted, whacking her brick at Adam with her fork.

"Blocked!" Adam yelled, knocking it back.

All the Second Besters joined in with their bricks.

We started a frenzy of stabbing and jabbing. I hit my brick so hard, it shot up four or five feet. As it tumbled down, Mookie leaped from his seat and tried to spear it in midair. His fork glanced off the edge of the pizza, sending it flying past my ear.

Mookie kept coming. He toppled forward, the fork still gripped in his fist. Luckily, I stopped his fall.

With my face.

I stared down. My eyes crossed as I looked at his hand. And then I followed the blurred, shiny thing that was between his fist and my nose.

The fork handle . . .

In my face . . .

I screamed. Mookie tumbled backward like he'd just jammed the fork in an electric outlet. He did a half flip over his chair, landing flat on the floor.

I yanked the fork, but it was stuck. Past my clenched fist, I could see Abigail staring at me from the Table of the Doomed. She looked like she was watching a horror movie. Mookie, sprawled on the ground, looked like he was a victim in a horror movie. Everyone else at my table was staring at him.

I leaped from my seat and raced to the boys' room at the end of the hall. I crashed through the door, ran over to the row of sinks, and stared at myself in the mirror.

The two tines in the middle of the fork were sunk into the center of my nose. The two tines on the outside speared through my nostrils. I could have been the lead singer in a punk rock band. I was definitely screaming like one.

The sight totally freaked me out. I tugged at the fork. It wouldn't budge. I pulled harder. No luck.

The door swung open. "Oh man," Mookie said. "I was hoping I didn't stick you too badly, but that looks really deep. It's got to hurt."

I started to nod, but then I stopped dead as the weird truth hit me: *It didn't hurt.*

"It's all my fault," Mookie said. "I'm the worst best friend in the world. Or the best worst friend. I'm sorry. I wasn't trying to stab you."

"I know. Forget about that. Just help me get it out."

Mookie tucked his index finger against his thumb, reached out, then flicked the end of the fork. It vibrated, making a *wubba-wubba-wubba* sound. "Cool. Sort of like the tuning forks in music class." He flicked it again, harder.

"Stop that!"

"Sorry. I just gotta work my way up to this. It's not

every day you get asked to un-fork someone." Mookie grabbed the fork and pulled. It didn't budge. He grabbed it with both hands, put one foot against my chest, and yanked.

That did the trick.

The fork pulled free with a grating sound I don't ever want to hear again. Mookie toppled over. I staggered back and slammed into the wall behind me.

The door opened again, and Principal Ambrose walked in. He stared at us. I was standing there with my hand clamped over my nose. Mookie was on his back with a fork in his hand. I wanted to say something, but my mind was coming up empty.

The principal shook his head. "I don't even want to know what this is about. Just get back to wherever you belong." As he headed out, he muttered, "One more year, and then I retire."

I checked my nose in the mirror. There were four tiny red holes in my face. A little dribble of blood leaked from each hole. I grabbed a paper towel and washed my face.

"Nate, are you sure you're okay?" Mookie asked.

"I don't know. It doesn't hurt. Shouldn't it hurt? . . ."

"Maybe you're in shock," Mookie said. "Like once, I read about a guy who lost both arms in an accident, and managed to carry them to the hospital. Wait—something about that story doesn't sound right."

"Let's just get back to the cafeteria," I said. "Anybody notice what happened?"

"I don't think so. It's way too loud in there to hear any screams." Mookie held up the fork. "Man, that's a lot of blood."

I leaned toward the mirror. The bleeding had stopped. "That's not blood. It's pizza sauce. Blood's not that lumpy."

"I thought it was a clot or something." Mookie sniffed the fork. Then he licked it. "You're right. Yum. Good sauce. Come on—now I'm starving."

Back at the cafeteria, the Second Besters looked like they'd been on the losing side of a paintball battle. They were so busy scrubbing sauce off their shirts with wet paper towels that they didn't pay any attention to me.

But someone else did. Before I could slip back into my seat, Abigail rushed up to me. "Are you okay?" She had a bunch of napkins in one hand and a piece of ice in the other. "I know first aid."

"What are you talking about? I don't need first aid."

"But you had a fork in your nose."

"It wasn't deep." I'm not sure why I was lying. Maybe because I really didn't want to think about it myself.

Mookie started to speak. "Actually, it was—"

I grabbed my pizza brick and jammed it in his mouth. As he chomped down, I turned back to Abigail. I needed to talk to her uncle about my numb tongue. I needed to know why I could get burned and stabbed without feeling any pain. All of this had started when I'd gotten splashed with Hurt-Be-Gone. Abigail's uncle was the only person who might be able to explain it. And fix it.

"Is your uncle in jail?" I wasn't sure whether the cops would let a kid visit someone they'd locked up.

"He's not in jail anymore," Abigail said.

"Good." I figured I could go see him right after school.

"No, it isn't good," she said.

"Why not?"

"He escaped from the police station right after they got there. He's on the run."

"He can't be."

Abigail shrugged. "With Uncle Zardo, he pretty much can't *not* be. It's sort of his nature to flee."

"No. You don't understand. I really need to talk to him. You have to get in touch with him. Okay?" I grabbed her shoulders. "Please. You'll try. Right?"

"Sure. Calm down. I'll try."

"Promise?"

"Cross my heart."

"Great. Call me as soon as you hear from him."

Abigail nodded and scurried back to her table.

"What was that about?" Mookie asked.

I pulled him away from our table, then leaned toward him and whispered, "I think the Hurt-Be-Gone messed me up big-time. That's why I need to talk to Abigail's uncle."

Mookie wiped some sauce from his chin with the back of his hand. "Maybe it will wear off."

"What if it doesn't?" As that thought shot through my mind and took a thousand scary turns, I reached in my pocket for my inhaler. I pulled it out, and froze.

"What's wrong?" Mookie asked.

"My lungs feel fine." For the first time in my life, even though I was upset, I didn't need my inhaler. That really scared me.

6

The Inversion Diet

N ot hungry?" **Mom** asked as I picked at my chicken that night. Dad had stopped on the way home from work to grab a bucket of wings for dinner. He does that a lot when Mom starts talking about making zucchini lasagna.

"Not really." Normally, I could eat a dozen wings and still have room for a couple bowls of cookie-dough ice cream. Right then, I would've had trouble eating a couple hummingbird thighs. I hadn't been hungry all day. That was weird, because food was one of my favorite things—especially when it wasn't prepared by either of my parents. If this kept up, I might actually end up being the skinniest kid in school. Though I'd probably have to avoid food for at least a month to give Gervaise "The Twig" Halleck any competition.

"Are you getting sick?" Mom felt my forehead. "You're chilled! Oh dear, I knew you were coming down with something. I'd better take your temperature."

"I'm fine." I pulled back as it hit me that my temperature might not be normal. "They had pizza for lunch. The slices were huge. Can I save the chicken for later?"

"I guess . . . ," Mom said.

I sat there while my parents ate, and stared down at the pieces of meat on my plate. Dead meat. I was starting to think that the chicken wings and I had a lot in common.

After dinner, I called Abigail. She didn't answer.

That night, I kept thinking about that fork sinking into my nose. Maybe Mookie was right. I could be in some sort of shock from the accident. My brain might have switched off. But I hadn't felt the hot pan, either. And my tongue was still numb.

Midnight came and went. I still couldn't sleep. I turned on my light and did the next couple days' worth of math homework. Then I read five chapters of social studies. Even that didn't put me to sleep. It was nearly two o'clock now. I went downstairs and turned on the computer.

What to do?

I thought about that zombie game. Maybe I could

find some tips online, and prove to everyone that I wasn't a total vidiot loser. I started to search. I found a bunch of sites with hints and walk-throughs, but I also stumbled across a PC version of the game. Better yet, you could try the first level for free.

Dad always warned me to be careful about downloading anything. But the game came right from the company Web site, and our virus checker said it was okay.

It took almost fifteen minutes to download, and another ten to install. So I didn't start playing until around two thirty.

I set it for EASY. The PC version was pretty much the same as the handheld one, which meant I got killed right away. Normally, that's when I'd start feeling all nervous and distracted. I held up my hand and stared at it. I wasn't shaky at all. My hand wasn't sweaty, either. My second guy lasted longer. My third guy made it all the way to the first checkpoint. I was getting better.

The next thing I knew, it was three fifteen, and I'd beaten the first level. I bumped the difficulty up from EASY to NORMAL, and played again.

I got right through it. Maybe I really could prove I was better than everyone thought. I decided not to switch to HARD. Not yet. So I played through again at NORMAL. This time, I beat the level without losing a guy.

When the first bits of light crept across the floor, I got up from the computer, went to the kitchen, and watched the sun rise. I didn't really feel tired, even though I hadn't slept at all, so I went back to the computer and played some more. An hour later, I heard Mom and Dad get up. I slipped back in bed so Mom could wake me for breakfast.

"This should perk up your appetite," Mom said as she placed a plate in front of me.

I stared down at the waffle. After skipping dinner, I should have been starving. But the waffle might as well have been a piece of wood. I wasn't interested in food. I wasn't interested in anything except talking to Abigail's uncle.

"I'm going to get you an appointment with Dr. Scrivello," Mom said.

That was the last thing I wanted. Dr. Scrivello would definitely figure out there was something wrong with me, and then Mom would totally freak out. She'd probably put me in a sealed room or something. I had to keep her from getting suspicious.

"Mom, there's nothing wrong with me." I wondered whether any kid in the history of the world had ever told a bigger lie. I picked up my knife and fork, cut off a chunk of waffle, and forced myself to swallow it. Her frown relaxed a bit, but she was still staring at me. I ate another bite. By the time I'd choked down half the waffle, Mom seemed satisfied. So I got out of the house without being dragged to the doctor.

I searched for Abigail in front of the school, but she

wasn't there yet. Mookie was there, waiting for me next to the front steps. "You look awful," he said.

"Thanks, Mom," I said.

"You put on some weight, too." He poked my stomach. "You're going to lose your hold on second place. And face it, third-skinniest kid in the class is a pretty worthless title. Unless there are only three kids in the class. Because then you'd also be the fattest."

I looked down at my waist. I had to admit my stomach bulged a bit. I leaned from side to side and heard a sloshing sound. I guess I had to add one more symptom to my growing list. "I don't think I'm digesting my food."

"Ick. That's not good. It could start to rot. When's the last time you went to the bathroom?" Mookie asked.

I opened my mouth to answer him, and discovered I wasn't sure. Definitely not today. Maybe not yesterday. I started to tell this to Mookie, but what came out of my mouth was "*Uuuhhhbluuuupppppuuuhhhuuubooorrruppp.*"

The burp lasted about thirty seconds, though it seemed more like a lifetime.

Mookie's face paled, and he staggered back. "Man, I didn't know burps could stink so bad. Something's definitely rotting in your stomach. We have to get it out of you before you kill everyone."

I nodded and let out a smaller burp. It lasted only about fifteen seconds. I waited to see if there was any more coming, but it looked like that was all the excess gas I had for the moment. "How am I going to do that?"

"Stick your finger down your throat," Mookie said.

"Good idea." I didn't want to throw up where people would see me. That's the sort of thing that can earn a kid a nickname that stays with him for years. There's no way I want to go through life as "Pukey Abercrombie." I led Mookie to the Dumpsters behind the school. Then I stuck my finger down my throat.

Nothing.

I didn't gag. I really couldn't tell my finger was there. The more I thought about all that food just lying around inside me, rotting like the bottom of a swamp, the more I panicked. Some of it was probably sitting there since Friday or Saturday. I needed to get it out as soon as possible. "Maybe if I hang upside down."

"Let's go inside," Mookie said. "We'll find something you can hang from."

I followed him through the side door and down the hall to the gym. He peeked in, then headed over to the parallel bars and said, "Try hanging down from these."

Great. Gymnastics equipment and I didn't get along very well. But I was ready to try anything. I got up on the bars, hooked my knees over them, then hung upside down. My stomach moved like a gigantic water balloon.

"Now what?"

"Open your mouth and wait, I guess." Mookie said. "The food should fall right out."

It didn't. "We need to try something else." My mind went racing through all sorts of ways to empty my stomach. I pictured myself swallowing a garden hose or taking a wild ride on a playground merry-go-round. I grabbed the bar so I could pull myself off.

"Hold still," Mookie said. "I think I know what to do." He reached out and pressed against my stomach. "I saw a vet on TV help a cow give birth this way. Or maybe it was a bull. No, wait. It had to be a cow."

I tried to tell him that was his stupidest idea ever. But the moment I opened my mouth, something plopped onto the floor.

"What was that?" I bent my head back as far as I could and tried to look at the floor, but it was hard for me to see anything in my position.

"You have waffles for breakfast?" Mookie asked.

"Yeah."

"You really need to learn to chew your food better. You could choke or something."

Mookie kept pressing. I didn't say anything more. My throat was busy with other tasks. The waffle was followed by more hunks of stuff and lots of liquid.

"Feel better?" Mookie asked when I got off the parallel bars.

"I don't feel anything." I stared at the mound of food. The sight should have at least made my stomach quiver a bit. I didn't feel sick at all. That scared me. There was more going on than just the fact that I didn't feel pain or digest my food. A whole bunch of parts of me had shut down. Important parts. At least I could see and hear. Unfortunately, I could also taste. Even with my numb tongue, I got far too good a lesson about the flavor of rotting food.

"You still don't feel anything at all?"

"Nope. That Hurt-Be-Gone must have messed up my nerves or something. It's not wearing off."

Mookie leaned closer to me and stared at my face.

"What's wrong?" I asked.

He stared for a long time before speaking. "I'm pretty sure it's worse than you think," he finally said. "A whole lot worse."

7

Gone, but Not Forgotten

What are you talking about?" I asked Mookie. "What could be worse than being totally numb and not digesting my food?"

"Being totally dead," he said.

I stared at him as his words sunk in. "I'm not dead. I can't be dead." I smacked him in the shoulder. "Could a dead person do that?" I smacked his other shoulder. "Could a dead person do THAT?" I kept smacking him. I was dangerously close to switching from his shoulder to his face.

"Ouch! Stop that. Listen to me for a minute. You

don't feel pain. You don't digest food. On top of that, I don't think you're breathing."

"Of course I'm breathing." I dropped my fists and wondered why I wasn't out of breath from smacking him. I'd played around with a punching bag at the YMCA once, and I'd started gasping after a couple minutes.

"Are you sure you're breathing?"

"Yeah." Even as I spoke, I realized I wasn't all that sure. I just assumed I was breathing, because I'd been breathing my whole life.

"Hang on," Mookie said. "There's one unbeatable test." He clenched his fists. His face scrunched up for a second so his cheeks and forehead swallowed his eyes. He looked like a badly made Play-Doh sculpture of himself. He grunted. Then his face relaxed. "Smell that?"

"Smell what?"

"Wow. If you don't smell that, you can't possibly be breathing." He fanned the air in front of his face. "You didn't smell your burp, either. Did you? And that was a real killer."

"I must have." But I had no memory of it.

"Let's make sure. Pinch your nose."

I pinched my nose and kept my mouth closed. I waited for that feeling—the one where your lungs start to scream for air, like the time I tried to swim all the way across the community pool underwater. My lungs didn't seem concerned, no matter how long I waited. I looked up at the clock behind the backboard and watched the minutes tick off.

Four ticks later, I let go of my nose. "I'm dead."

The words hung in the air, too large for me to really make sense of them. A wad of fear started to grow in my brain. But it was lonely fear—no trembles, twinges, or jittery butterflies—just fear itself. It looked like I could be afraid in my mind, but I couldn't feel fear in my body.

I dropped to the floor and put my head in my hands. "I'm really dead. This is it. Dead . . ."

Mookie dropped down next to me. "I don't want to go to a funeral. I'm scared of them."

"There isn't going to be any funeral," I said. "Nobody's sticking me in a coffin."

"I totally don't know what to do." He got up and started pacing. "Am I supposed to get you a present? Or maybe a card. I'm completely lost."

"Will you stop babbling? I'm the one with the problem."

"Hey," Mookie said. "This is hard for me, too."

"What do you mean?"

"Well, usually if a guy's friend dies, the guy gets all sorts of sympathy and stuff. And his teachers cut him a break. I could really use a break after my score on our last math test. I get the feeling I won't be enjoying any of that because you don't act like you're dead. I guess maybe you're half dead, which doesn't do either of us any good."

"Cheer up," I told him. "Maybe one of your other friends will die for real."

"I don't have any other friends."

"Well, maybe you can make friends with someone who's real sick, if sympathy is that important to you."

"Now you're making me sound selfish. I guess it's sort of worse for you than for me. I really am sorry. I wish you weren't dead."

I stared at my hands. They didn't look dead. I felt for my pulse. I couldn't find anything, but I was never very good at finding my pulse, anyhow. I still wasn't totally ready to accept that I was dead. "If I'm not breathing, how can I talk?"

"I don't know. Maybe you can suck in air when you want to say something. So your lungs work. They just don't work on their own. Try it."

I drew in a deep breath through my nose. Now I smelled something. "Oh man, Mookie. And you think *I'm* rotting inside? What did you eat last night?"

"Mom made pork and beans with sauerkraut and coleslaw. And onion soup. But this is great. You can make your lungs work. Like I said, you're not totally dead. Just sort of half dead. Maybe your heart can work, too. I'll bet we can start it back up."

I took another breath—through my mouth, to avoid a second helping of Mookie's toxic gas blast—and watched my ribs expand. "You really think we can get my heart going again?"

"Sure. I see them do it on TV all the time. They have one of those things in Mr. Lomux's office."

"What things?"

"Defiber-something . . ."

"Defibrillator?"

"Yeah. That's it. Come on."

I checked the gym clock again. It was almost time for the bell. I didn't care. If Mookie could get my heart going again, that would be the best thing that had ever happened to me.

I followed him into Mr. Lomux's office. The defibrillator was in the corner. It had a couple switches and a button. And all sorts of large red warning labels filled with exclamation points, lightning bolts, and pictures of skulls.

"This thing could kill someone," I said.

"So you've got nothing to worry about." Mookie flipped the main switch. A display showed the word CHARGING. Then it beeped and changed to READY.

"Take off your shirt," he said.

I took off my shirt. Then I stretched out on Mr. Lomux's desk.

"Ready?"

"Go for it."

He put the paddles against my chest and shouted, "CLEAR!"

"Why are you shouting?"

"That's what they do on TV."

"Forget that and just do it."

Mookie pushed the button.

Zzzzzap!

My body jolted so hard, I bounced on the desk. I put my hand on the side of my neck. No pulse. I pinched my palm. No pain. "Try again."

Mookie turned a dial to a higher setting and zapped me again. Nothing happened, except that the lights in the gym dimmed for a second. After the third try, Mookie sniffed, then said, "I smell bacon."

I looked down at my chest. Wisps of smoke rose from around the paddles. I pushed Mookie's hands away and slid off the desk. "That's enough." There were dark marks from the paddles. I brushed at them, and little bits of charred skin peeled off. I was almost glad I couldn't feel anything.

I put my shirt on as the first bell rang. "Come on. We don't want to be late."

"What do you care?" Mookie asked me. "You're dead. You can probably get out of school. Or at least, out of gym."

"Whatever is happening, I'm not ready to drop out of school." Or out of the human race. Maybe I was dead— or half dead—but I didn't plan to stay that way. I had too much living I still wanted to do.

"What's that?" Mookie asked.

"Footsteps!"

We ducked. I peeked into the gym through the office

66

window as someone came through the door on the other side of the bleachers. Oh great—I'd know those blue sweatpants anywhere. "It's Mr. Lomux."

He was headed right toward us. "Hey—who's in there. I see you. You can't hide from me. You kids are in big trouble."

He sprinted toward the office. I thought about making a run for it, but there was no way I could escape. He'd catch me before I reached the hallway. But as he ran past the parallel bars, his foot landed right in the slimy pile of food. His legs shot out from under him, and he went up in the air like a very uncoordinated high jumper.

If his leap was bad, his landing was even worse. He came down flat on his back. Mookie and I both winced at the sound of his head bouncing off the gym floor. Luckily, the soggy waffle chunks cushioned the blow a bit.

We ran out to the parallel bars. Mr. Lomux was staring up at the ceiling, but I had the feeling he wasn't seeing much of anything.

"He's breathing," Mookie said.

"Hard head," I said.

"Put me in, Coach," Mr. Lomux said. "I can score. I know I can. I won't drop the ball again. I promise."

Mookie leaned closer. "Wow, no veins popping. I guess he's finally found a way to relax."

I pulled Mookie away. "Let's get out of here."

We raced toward our class. The rest of the morning

went by without leaving much of an impression on me. My head was too full of the one huge idea I could no longer ignore.

I was dead. Oh man, if my mom found out, she'd kill me.

8

Brain Trust

I WAS SO late getting to class that I didn't have a chance to talk to Abigail right away. At lunch, I rushed over to her table. It felt weird approaching the Table of the Doomed. Fear flashed across a couple faces, and Ferdinand slid under the table. I realized that to some of them, anyone was a potential bully.

Abigail smiled at me from across the table and pointed at an empty seat. "Hi. Want to join us? There's lots of room."

"Did you talk with your uncle?"

"I sent him an e-mail. But I didn't hear back yet."

I smacked the table with my fist. "You have to find

him. I need to get in touch with him. Right away. Like now. Immediately. If not sooner."

"You're babbling," Abigail said. "What's wrong?"

"Nothing. Everything is fine. Absolutely perfect. Couldn't be better."

"Something's wrong. Maybe I can help," she said.

"Nothing's wrong!" I shouted. Snail Girl grabbed her lunch box and scurried to a different table. Ferdinand crawled out from his hiding place and slithered toward the door. The remaining kids turned away. "You can't help. Nobody can help."

"Aha! If nobody can help, then there has to be something that requires help. So something is wrong," Abigail said. "I knew it."

I felt like I'd been grabbed by a bulldog. My brain must be as dead as my body if Abigail was outsmarting me. She wasn't going to let go until I gave her an answer. I leaned forward, placed my hands on the table, and said the first thing that came to mind. "I think my parents are getting a divorce." It was a total lie, but I figured it would satisfy her.

"That's a total lie. If that was your problem, you wouldn't need to talk with my uncle." Abigail leaned across the table. "Something is wrong with you. You haven't blinked once since you got here. And you still have little holes in your nose from Mookie's fork."

"I'm a slow healer."

She leaned even closer. I could see small dark

flecks in her light brown eyes. "And you also don't feel pain."

"Are you crazy or something? Of course I feel pain."

Abigail moved back a step, then pointed at my arm. There was a fork stuck in it.

"Ow!" I leaped away, yanked out the fork, and pretended it hurt.

"Nice try," she said. "But you're a lousy actor. Come on. Just tell me the truth. Maybe I can help."

There was no point trying to hide this from her. Next, she'd probably stab me with a knife or smack me with a sledgehammer.

"Okay—ever since your uncle spilled that stuff on me . . ."

I stopped. I didn't want to say it again. I didn't want it to become real.

"I was afraid of this." Abigail came around the table and patted me on the back. "Take your time."

"Ever since I got splashed with Hurt-Be-Gone, I haven't felt anything. And I sort of don't seem to need to breathe. Or eat."

"No pulse, either." Mookie had walked up behind me. He slid his finger across his throat and made a slashing sound.

"And your uncle isn't here to tell me how to fix things," I said. "He's running around the country, hiding from the police. It's hopeless." I dropped down in a chair.

"Actually, by now he's probably out of the country. The last time he got in trouble this big, he hid out in Argentina for six months."

"Argentina? This just gets better and better." I banged my forehead on the table.

Hard.

It didn't hurt.

"It looks like it's up to me to help you," Abigail said.

"That's a nice offer," I said, "but I need a scientist."

"Uncle Zardo told me all about his work."

"Yeah, right . . ." I tried to find a way to say what I was thinking without hurting her feelings.

Mookie erased that problem by blurting out what he was thinking. "Come on, Abigail, you're too stupid to understand science."

She ignored him. "You don't think I'm very smart, do you, Nathan?"

There was no safe answer to that question. Abigail kept staring at me. Finally, I said, "You don't even take notes in class."

"That's because I don't need to."

"Yeah, right," Mookie said.

"What did we talk about in math this morning?" she asked him.

"Something about numbers," Mookie said. "I'm pretty sure numbers were involved. Lots of them. Big numbers. Or maybe it was small ones. Or both. That's it. Both."

"To make a mixed fraction from an improper fraction, use division." Abigail turned back toward me. "What about science?"

"Plant stuff," I said. "Producing food from sunlight." That was as much as I remembered.

"Photosynthesis," Abigail said. "Plants use chlorophyll to convert solar energy and carbon dioxide to food, producing oxygen as a by-product."

She kept going. "In social studies, we learned about the Louisiana Purchase, which happened in 1803. During opening announcements, they played a selection from a Haydn string quartet, which he wrote in 1793. The first five prints on the wall of the art room, next to the door, are by Chagall, Picasso, Escher, Bookbinder, and Cassatt. Enough? Did I prove my point?"

"Yeah . . ." I stared at her, trying to see Abigail as a really smart kid, and not the slacker I thought she was. "But, why?"

"Smart girls get picked on," she said. "A girl can be pretty. A girl can be athletic. But if she's smart, she's treated like a freak. Kindergarten and first grade were a nightmare for me until I learned that. Nobody was interested in the stuff I wanted to talk about. Everyone mocked me. Besides, what do you think my life would be like if I knocked Eddy Mason out of his spot as the smartest kid in the class?"

"Rotten," I said. Eddy wasn't just smart. He was also mean, and very competitive. I could imagine what he'd do to Abigail if she dethroned him.

73

"You bet. So, I sit in class and I learn what they teach, but I don't show off. I'll save that for college."

A small glimmer of hope shone through the layers of doom that had fallen on me. "Are you smart enough to help me?"

"I'm smart enough to be your best chance," she said.

I turned toward Mookie. "What do you think?"

"One question," he said.

"What?" Abigail asked.

"Would you do my homework for me?"

9

Back to the Lab

We headed for the lab right after school.
"Are you sure we can just walk right in? Even
if your uncle isn't there?"

"No problem," Abigail said. "It's a community college. It's open to the public."

Sure enough, we went right up to the lab. The door
was unlocked. Everything was just the way we'd left it.

"Now we need to find Uncle Zardo's notes." Abigail
headed across the room to a computer.

I watched over her shoulder as she scrolled through
a bunch of files. Then I turned my attention to keeping
Mookie from playing with the bottles of chemicals on

the shelves, or any of the dangerous-looking lab instruments on the tables. Just as I was prying his hands off some kind of high-powered blender, and explaining to him that there really wasn't any way we could use it to make milk shakes right now, Abigail shouted, "Got it!"

I ran back over to her. "What'd you find?"

"I know his main ingredient. Ohmygosh! He's using something called the corpse flower."

"That doesn't sound good," I said.

"It isn't. No wonder he got in trouble. It's a protected species. He was supposed to be using the corpus flower. It's entirely different."

"How do you know that?" I asked.

Abigail looked out the window. Then she looked at the floor. Then she said, "I sort of helped him come up with the formula."

"Sort of?" I knew she was smart, but I couldn't imagine what kind of help she could give a scientist.

"I guess I actually helped him a whole lot. To tell the truth, it was all my idea. Except for using the wrong ingredient. I love neurobiology."

"What are you—some kind of scientific genius?" I asked.

"I guess that would be an accurate description. Though I don't like to brag. Anyhow, we didn't come here to talk about me. I'm pretty sure your problem is caused by the corpse flower. According to what I just read, it has some properties that aren't very well understood. It comes from a place called Bezimo Island, way out in the Atlantic Ocean."

"Never heard of it," I said. "Have you?"

"No. I'm going to need to do more research. And then I'm going to need to run some simulations of the relevant molecules on the computer. Some proteins are incredibly complex. This could take awhile. Why don't I meet up with you guys later?"

"Sure. Where?"

"Your place?" she asked. "My place is a bit messy right now."

"Okay." I told her my address. Then Mookie and I headed out.

"Who'd ever have guessed that Abigail was so smart," Mookie said. "She did a great job hiding it. I wonder if she's hiding her height, too. Maybe she's just pretending to be that short. If she's really smart, she could probably figure out a way to do that. Optical illusions, or mirrors. Maybe even lasers."

By the time we got to my house, Mookie had convinced himself that half the kids in our class were hiding something. I guess I couldn't really argue, at least as far as my own secret.

We headed up the stairs to my room. "Beat you there," Mookie shouted. As he squeezed past, he accidentally stomped on my foot.

"Ouch!"

Ouch?

I hobbled to the top of the stairs, then looked at my foot. "I felt that. Maybe the Hurt-Be-Gone is wearing off." If that was true, it would be great.

"Let's see." Mookie stomped on my other foot.

"Yeouch! Stop that."

"You're cured. Yay—I helped." He threw his hands in the air and did a victory dance. "I cured Nathan, I cured Nathan. I'm a hero, I'm a hero."

I ran my hands down my legs. I had no feeling until right below my knees. Everything above that was dead. The weirdest part was touching my living legs with my dead hands.

"It only splashed on my upper body," I said. "It's not wearing off. I think it's spreading." I had no idea how quickly that was happening. I went into my room, rolled up my pants leg, ran my fingernail across my skin until I found the exact place where I could first feel anything, and drew a line with a black marker.

"Tattoos!" Mookie said. "Awesome. Draw one on me."

I gave him one while we waited. At least it stopped him from dancing.

Abigail rang my bell an hour later. She was panting, like she'd jogged all the way from the college. "I've got good news and bad news," she said.

10

▼

Tipping the Scales

What's the good news?" I asked.

"There's a cure."

I wanted to jump and shout, but I needed to hear the rest. "And the bad news?"

"The cure only works if the transformation isn't complete."

"That's great," I said. "My legs are still alive."

"Watch." Mookie stomped on my toe. "See?"

"Ow! Stop that!" I limped away from him before he decided to give Abigail more evidence.

"Cool," Mookie said. "You really look like a zombie when you limp."

"I'm not a zombie!" I yelled.

"Sure you are," Mookie said.

"Zombies rise from the dead," I said. "They eat brains. They drool. They snarl and growl. I'm not a zombie!"

"The brain thing is from the movies," Abigail said. "According to myth, zombies rise from the dead. But according to science, living people can be turned into zombies."

Mookie reached out and touched my chin. "No drool. But you're sort of snarling."

"Knock it off," I said.

I didn't feel like arguing about zombies. I was more interested in the cure. I expected Abigail to be happy that I wasn't totally dead. Instead, she said, "I guess you'll want to hear the other bad news."

"Not really." I'd had a lifetime's worth of bad news in the last couple days. "But go ahead."

"The cure is only available on Bezimo Island. You know, the place where the corpse flower comes from."

"How far away is that?" I asked.

"One thousand six hundred thirty-five miles," Abigail said.

My heart sank as soon as I heard the word *thousand*.

"Can we order it on the Internet?" Mookie asked.

Abigail shook her head. "The cure is made from the scales of a rare tropical fish called the Lazarus mullet. It's not exactly something people sell online."

"People sell everything online," Mookie said. "My

mom bought an autographed photo of Julius Caesar. It's a collector's item."

Abigail and I both stared at him for a moment, but neither of us bothered to point out the problem with that.

"You can't use some other fish?" I asked.

"No," Abigail said. "It has to be that one."

I flopped down on my bed. "It's over. I'm doomed."

"You mean, you're dead," Mookie said.

"Right. Thanks for pointing that out." My feet throbbed where Mookie had stomped them. I realized that as long as I still had any feeling, I couldn't give up. There had to be some way to get the cure. "What about an aquarium? Would there be one of those fish there?"

"That's not a bad idea." Abigail looked around my room. "Where's your computer?"

"I don't have my own." I led her downstairs to the family room. "We all have to share it."

Two steps into the room, Abigail froze. "Why do you have so many dead plants?"

"It's my Mom's hobby." I was so used to it, I never paid much attention to the dried brown leaves and wilted stalks. There were three shelves filled with flower pots along the wall next to the window. The pots were filled with plants, most of which were not looking very healthy. There was a whole shelf of plant stuff in the garage, too. "She loves to raise plants, but she's so busy at work that she doesn't have a lot of time for that kind of stuff. And she sort of forgets to water them. I call it 'death row.'"

Abigail shuddered, then sat at the computer. I walked over to the shelves and examined the latest victims. Sometimes, when a plant was mostly dead, Mom would cut off the living part and replant it. There were a couple of those survivors on the bottom shelf, totally unaware that their doom was just being delayed.

"I guess it's a good thing your Mom doesn't want to raise kittens or puppies," Mookie said. "You're lucky she didn't let you dry up when you were little—or starve to death."

"The way my mom cooks, that might have been less cruel."

About a minute later, Abigail said, "Hey, they have a Lazarus mullet at the Hurston Aquarium."

"That's not far," Mookie said.

Abigail scrolled the Web page. "They're open late tonight."

"It's nowhere near the bus routes. How are we going to get there?" I asked. "My parents are working."

"My mom lost her license," Mookie said. "And Dad doesn't know how to drive."

"Can your mom take us?" I asked Abigail.

"Our van's kind of messy," she said.

"And I'm kind of dead," I said. "And it's kind of your fault."

"Good point. I'll call my mom. Just promise not to say anything about the mess."

I left a note for my parents, telling them I was doing a school project. Abigail grabbed a plastic bag from my kitchen and asked me to find a pair of tweezers.

"Are you sure there's no easier cure?" I asked while we waited for her mom.

"I'm sure. A solution isn't like a piece of clothing. You can't always find one that fits the way you want."

Fifteen minutes later, Abigail, Mookie, and I were seated in the back of Mrs. Goldberg's van, flying down the highway toward the Hurston Aquarium. We were sort of wedged in the middle row. The back was crammed with magazines, cans, boxes, and bags. I couldn't even tell whether there was a seat under the stuff. There were even a couple small appliances, including a Crock-Pot with a frayed power cord, an old toaster with a cracked case, and a vacuum cleaner with a broken handle.

"I'm so happy my little Abigail has some school friends," Mrs. Goldberg said. "She spends far too much time up in her room with her books. I've been telling her for years that she needs to learn to be more social, or she'll end up like her uncles. Those men just don't do well in the real world."

Abigail shot her mother a frown, but it seemed to go unnoticed. Next to me, Mookie thumbed through a stack of magazines that looked like they'd been published before we were born. "So, you collect stuff?" he asked.

I rammed him with an elbow, but Mrs. Goldberg just said, "Oh, certainly. I can't bear to throw out something that might come in handy someday. People are so wasteful, it's a shame. Everything is a treasure to someone."

She pulled up to the entrance of the aquarium and said, "I need to go to the recycling center. I'll be back here in two hours to pick you youngsters up. Have fun."

"Now what?" I asked Abigail as her mom pulled away.

"Simple. We find the fish. Then you sneak into the tank and pluck a couple scales from it. Don't worry—you won't hurt the fish." Abigail handed me the plastic bag.

It didn't sound simple. But I was ready to do whatever I had to. I paid for our tickets and we went in. I was glad the place wasn't crowded.

"It's in the tropical tank," Abigail said after she'd checked the guidebook.

The tropical tank filled one huge wall of a room just past the main hall. It must have been twenty or thirty feet long. I stared at what seemed to be a half-million different fish. "How will we spot it?"

"That's the one." Abigail pointed to a pudgy brown lump resting on the bottom. All the other fish were bright and lively. It figured that mine would be dull and lifeless.

"Are you sure it's not dead?" I asked.

Abigail leaned closer to the glass. "It's alive. Its gills are moving."

"So Nathan is less alive than a mullet," Mookie said.

"Thanks for reminding me."

The tank went all the way to the ceiling. There was no opening on this side.

I guess Abigail knew what I was thinking. "There has to be an opening so they can feed the fish." She pointed to a door marked EMPLOYEES ONLY. "Try there."

"What if someone comes in?" I asked.

"I can fix that." Mookie scrunched his face and started to hunch over.

"No, stop!" I put a hand on his shoulder. I didn't think Abigail could survive one of his toxic gas clouds. "That's okay. I'll risk it."

I glanced around, made sure nobody was about to come in from the main hall, then slipped through the door. I found myself in a narrow passage along the side of the tank. I followed it around to the back. A long ladder rose all the way to the top of the tank, about fifteen feet over my head. I started to climb the ladder, then realized I didn't want to get my clothes wet. I took off my pants and shirt, but I kept my underwear on. There was no way I was going anywhere without that.

I paused at the top of the ladder. I knew I didn't need to breathe. I could stay underwater as long as I wanted. But by actually doing something no living person could do, I was sort of really admitting that I was dead. But if I didn't do something about it, I'd end up being dead forever.

"I won't get cured if I just stand here," I muttered.

I took a deep breath, even though I didn't need it, and slipped over the edge. The water felt warm against my feet and shins, but the rest of my body didn't notice anything.

My brain noticed everything. As soon as my head went under the water, it was like a timer went off in my mind, telling me I could hold my breath for only thirty or forty seconds. After a moment, I wanted to get out of the water. I remembered what it felt like to inhale a lungful of water. Or to choke on a drink. My brain was sure I'd need to draw a breath, but my body didn't play along.

Relax. You don't need to breathe.

I'm underwater.

You can stay here all day.

But I'll drown.

You can't drown. You're already dead.

"Enough!" I shouted. Bubbles shot past my face. Water rushed into my mouth. I didn't drown. I didn't choke. I didn't need to cough.

I swam down toward the Lazarus mullet. *This is actually kind of cool.* I saw Mookie and Abigail on the other side. I opened my mouth and grinned at them. I stuck out my tongue. I closed my mouth and bulged out my cheeks. Then I tapped my wrist, like I was wearing a watch, and shrugged.

Mookie started laughing. Then he bulged out his cheeks. Abigail glanced over her shoulder and waved her hands frantically. I waved back and shouted, "Hi!"

She shook her head and said something. I watched her lips move. I still didn't get it.

Abigail breathed on the glass, fogging it up. Then she wrote ƎꓷIH..

I frowned. Abigail wiped the word out with the side of her fist, then fogged the glass again and wrote *HIDE*.

As a group of Brownies swarmed up to the tank, I swam behind a large chunk of coral. The instant the Brownies left, I swam over to the Lazarus mullet. When I got close, it rolled its eyes toward me. I waited, afraid it would try to escape. But it looked away, like I wasn't worth watching. I reached out with the tweezers and plucked a couple scales. It didn't even react. I was pretty sure that fish don't feel stuff the way that people do.

Then again, neither did I.

I put the scales in a plastic bag, then swam back to the ladder. I figured it would be a good idea to empty my lungs. I hung over the tank for a moment, pressing my body against the edge. Water ran out of my nose and mouth. After I climbed down, I stood behind the tank and dripped for a while.

I was just about to put on my pants when I heard the door open. A guy dressed in green overalls came in, carrying a bucket. I could see him through the glass. He hadn't noticed me, yet. But there was no way he wouldn't spot me when he came around to the back of the tank. I was about to get caught standing in an employees-only area in my underwear, clutching a plastic bag with a stolen fish scale.

I looked for another way out, but there weren't any other doors. I was trapped. I grabbed the ladder and wondered whether I had time to get back in the tank and hide.

That's when I heard a scream tear through the open door.

11

▽

Keep Your Chin Up

Shark!"

I looked through the tank. It was like watching a television that had way too much blue in the picture. But the show was definitely an action comedy. Mookie was running around in front of the tank, waving his arms in terror and screaming. "Help! Shark!"

The guy dropped the bucket and ran toward him. Mookie kept screaming as he raced into the next room. The guy chased after him.

"Knock it off, kid!"

I jumped into my clothes and went back through the door.

"Got it?" Abigail asked.

"Yup."

"Maybe we'd better leave. We can meet Mookie in the parking lot."

"Good idea." We went outside, and I handed her the bag.

"Great. That's plenty. Now we just have to mix it with the other ingredients and let it sit."

"Sit? How long?" I'd figured she'd whip up some kind of formula right away.

"I'm not sure. At least overnight. I have to extract the collagen fibrils from the calcium salts."

"We need to hurry. Can't you do it faster?" I could almost feel death creeping down my legs.

"You'll be fine," Abigail said.

"And don't come back until you learn how to behave!"

I looked over at the door, where Mookie was being ejected from the aquarium.

"Thanks," I said when he joined us. "You really saved me. I owe you one."

"Just keep that in mind when you become mindless and get an urge to eat brains."

"I'm not going to eat brains!" I shouted.

"I've got two kidneys," Mookie said. "I guess you could have one of those. But not my liver. I'm pretty sure I only have one. You probably wouldn't want it, anyhow. I'll bet even zombies don't eat liver."

I stopped listening.

When Mrs. Goldberg picked us up, she had even more stuff crammed in the van. I guess she went to the recycling center for the opposite reason than most people do. We wedged ourselves in and rode back to town.

"Thanks for the ride," I said when Mrs. Goldberg pulled up at my house.

"I'll get right to work on our science project." Abigail gave me a wink to let me know she meant the cure.

"We have a science project?" Mookie screamed. "Nobody told me. When's it due?"

I pushed him out of the van. "He's such a kidder," I said to Mrs. Goldberg.

I got out and waved as they drove off.

"It's great that Abigail is helping you," Mookie said after I'd explained to him that he wasn't about to flunk science.

"Yeah. I just wish I didn't have to wait for the cure. My parents are going to get suspicious if I don't eat dinner." I could see my mom dragging me to all sorts of doctors.

"That's no problem," Mookie said. "Just do what I do when my mom makes macaroni with clams and cheese. I push my food around and pretend I'm chewing something. The real trick is that I squish everything to one side so half my plate is empty. She never notices that I don't put anything in my mouth."

"That's not a bad idea. I'll give it a try."

Sure enough, I was able to get through dinner without actually eating. Since Mom had made fish cakes, I was especially happy I didn't have to put anything in my mouth.

Once again, I couldn't fall asleep. It looked like being awake was part of being dead, which was weird since people are always comparing death to sleep.

I went down to the computer and played the zombie game. This time, I put it on the hardest setting. No problem. I guess I had a couple things going for me. I never got nervous. No matter how exciting or tense the action got, my hand was steady. And I never blinked. I was a perfect game-playing machine. But I had only one sample level of the game, and I was getting tired of beating it.

I searched around for other game samples. There were plenty. If nothing else, it looked like I wouldn't be bored at night.

I used Mookie's trick at breakfast. It worked just as well as it had at dinner. Waffles are really easy to smush together so they take up less space on the plate.

"I'm glad you have your appetite back," Mom said as I put my knife and fork through the motions.

I was glad I wouldn't have to choke down a waffle and then return to the parallel bars. After I dumped the food from my plate into the garbage, I grabbed my backpack and headed out.

I raced up to Abigail as soon as I spotted her coming

down the sidewalk toward the school yard. "Got it?" I asked.

She gave me a funny look.

"What's wrong?"

"The process is slower than I'd expected. How much farther has the deadness moved?" she asked.

I pulled up my pants leg and showed her the latest mark, halfway down my shin.

"That's not too bad. We have time. I did some more research. We need another ingredient. But it won't be hard to find."

"Oh, that's just great," I moaned. "What do we need? A rare bird that lives in the Arctic?"

"A mushroom. But nothing rare. I'm pretty sure the one we need grows in Ackerman's Woods. We can go there after school."

"You didn't say anything about a mushroom yesterday."

"This process is extremely complicated. It's so near the far edge of science that it's almost like some kind of magic. Not that I believe in magic."

I didn't want to hear about science or magic. "Abigail, I'm trusting you with my life. Or my death. Or something like that."

"Don't worry, Nathan," she said. "I won't let you down."

As if there wasn't enough stress in my life, today was field day. We were about to spend the entire day competing against the kids from Perrin Hall Academy.

When we got out to the field, I saw Mort Ivanson on crutches. "What happened?" I asked.

"I heard he tripped on the steps yesterday," Mookie said.

"That's bad. He was our best hope."

"At least we still have Tammi." Mookie pointed at the track. "She's as fast as Mort."

Tammi Andrews was jogging warm-up laps. Rodney jogged up next to her. Then Rodney stumbled. He and Tammi went down in a tangle. Rodney sprang right up. But Tammi stayed on the ground, clutching her knee.

I watched Rodney closely while people ran over to help. He looked happy. I guess he'd decided to improve his chances of winning. I wondered whether he'd given Mort a push, too.

"We'll never beat Perrin Hall now," Mookie said.

"At least I won't get blamed for the loss." I checked the list and saw that Mookie and I were both scheduled for the broad jump first. Dead or alive, I was pretty bad at jumping. We went over and got in line. There were only three kids ahead of us, so it wasn't a long wait.

As I ran toward the pit for my first attempt, I realized I didn't have any nervous twinges. I was always afraid I'd hurt myself if I jumped too far. Right now, my gut couldn't care less what the rest of my body did.

I can't get hurt.

That thought helped launch me into the air. It was a magnificent leap, just like those track stars do in the

Olympics. I flew farther than I'd ever jumped before. I was half kid, half cat. But my first thought was followed, mid-jump, by a darker one.

I can still break something.

All my gracefulness vanished. I clutched at the air and tried to slow myself down. That didn't work. I lost my balance and toppled.

"Safe!" Mookie shouted, waving his arms like a third-base umpire as I landed flat on my stomach.

"Very funny," I said as I spat out sawdust.

I took it easy in the high jump. Then, when my turn came, I lined up for the mile. Rodney was next to me. At least I didn't have to worry about him tripping me. I wasn't any threat to him.

By the end of the first lap, I was in last place. But then I started to gain on everyone. At the end of the next lap, I was in the middle of the pack. By the third lap, I was right behind the leaders. I wasn't any faster than before, but I wasn't out of breath. I didn't need to slow down. My speed wasn't great for the first lap, but it was really good for the last one, when everyone else was running out of air.

The track seemed to glide beneath my feet. I found my rhythm and sailed through the final stretch. I almost didn't want to stop when I crossed the finish line. I never knew that running could be fun.

A girl from Perrin Hall came in first. But I took second, right ahead of a boy and another girl from Perrin

Hall. Rodney actually managed fifth place. He picked up a lot more points in the weight-lifting events, and moved into the top four. It didn't help—Perrin Hall was killing us on team points. Mr. Lomux wasn't even watching anymore. He was slumped on the bleachers with his head in his hands. We were so far behind, it was pretty much hopeless by the time I got to my last event.

I jumped up, grabbed the bar, and did my first chin-up. Mookie grabbed the bar next to me.

What's the point? I thought. So what if you could run faster than anyone else or jump higher? It didn't make you a better person. It sure didn't mean that everyone should treat you special or different. But everyone would go all wild over the winners.

I glanced at Mookie. He was slowing down. I wasn't surprised that I was lasting longer—I was a lot lighter.

Mookie hung from the bar, his face grew red, and then it became a scary darker shade that was somewhere between purple and blue. He groaned like someone was removing his appendix with a fork. Finally, he dropped, and landed with a loud "Ooff!"

One of the teachers, Mr. Bierce, who was counting for him, looked at the counter in his hand, and then said, "Three."

"Three?" Mookie asked. "I was sure I did at least ten."

"Three," Mr. Bierce said again. "And the last one was a gift. You barely got your forehead past the bar."

"Oh well. It's still a new record for me." Mookie flexed

his muscles, then wandered over next to my counter, Ms. Nurmi.

I kept going. I'd expected the whole day to be a nightmare. But my living nightmare actually made field day a lot more fun. Not that I'd trade my normal life for my new abilities. I was dying to find that mushroom so Abigail could finish the cure.

"Psssst."

I looked down at Mookie. He was trying to get my attention, but I wasn't sure why. He pointed at the counter in Ms. Nurmi's hand, then mouthed some words.

I had no idea what he was trying to tell me. I shrugged, which isn't easy when you're hanging from a bar.

"Two hundred and thirty-nine," Mookie said.

Oh, gosh. I froze in the middle of what was about to become my 240th chin-up. I hadn't realized I'd done so many. My arms weren't tired at all.

I dangled from the bar and looked around. Everyone was watching me. Including Rodney. He didn't look happy. I had to stop.

I started to pull myself up again, groaned, thrashed my legs, twisted violently, and then let go. I heard a snap as I fell from the bar. I dropped to my knees and gasped like I was exhausted.

As I got back to my feet, Mookie whispered, "Nice acting." He gave me a thumbs-up.

"Thanks." I held up my thumb. It wobbled, then

flopped over. I stared at it in horror for a moment, then straightened it out. I flexed it, and it seemed to work okay.

"Two hundred thirty-nine," Ms. Nurmi said. "My word, that's an impressive performance, young man. You've obviously been training very hard." She went over to the big score sheet taped to the back wall of the school and gave my count to the kids keeping track of the results.

I moved closer, so I could read my total. The next highest chin-up number I saw was forty-seven. And the highest-placed kid had 534 total points. Oh boy. I'd earned 478 points just for the chin-ups. Added to my other totals, that put me at 822. And it put Belgosi ahead of Perrin Hall.

As I was staring at the score, Mr. Lomux came over. I expected him to accuse me of cheating—or maybe of leaving undigested food on the gym floor. Instead, he smiled, patted my shoulder, and said, "Nice job, Abercrombie. I knew you'd come through if I gave you a push."

"Thanks." I was so startled, I said it about a minute after he'd walked away.

"Wow, his veins pop when he's really happy, too," Mookie said. "Looks like you'll be a captain."

"That's the last thing I care about."

"How'd you do it?" Mookie asked.

"I have no idea."

"Muscle fatigue occurs from depletion of anaerobic

energy sources," Abigail said as she walked up to us. "Living muscles get tired after a certain amount of exertion. It looks like dead muscles don't. There are probably all sorts of things you can do that a normal person can't. It's a shame we won't be able to explore all those possibilities. It would be fascinating to run some experiments."

"Yeah, I'm really sorry I can't stay dead for longer," I told her. "Maybe you can find another victim after you're done with me."

They called me over for the award ceremony. It was unreal. They even had a platform in front of the bleachers, like in the Olympics. I stood at the top. Our whole school cheered. Except for one person. Rodney glared at me and punched his palm. But the Second Besters and the Doomed went wild. Everyone started chanting, "Nathan! Nathan!" Shawna, Lexi, Talissa, Bekkah, and Cydnie were clapping and bouncing.

As much as I was eager to go to the woods and get the rest of the cure, I wasn't in a hurry to leave the awards ceremony. Maybe being half dead wasn't all bad.

12

▼

Shroooooom!

Abigail's mom dropped us off in the parking lot by the east side of Ackerman's Woods. "It's so nice you kids want to go for a hike. Most young people just care about video games and loud music. Or they stay in their rooms reading books. I'll be back at five thirty."

Abigail dashed ahead, then stopped and waited until we caught up. "I love the woods. Don't you?"

"I was a Boy Scout," Mookie said. "Well, actually, I was a Cub Scout. Sort of. I was going to join, but they didn't have a uniform my size. I was a lot bigger when I was little."

"What's this mushroom look like?" I asked.

"It's small, with a silvery brown cap and white spots. It mostly grows in the shade. I think I know a good area to search." She reached into her backpack. "I brought chocolate. It's the perfect energy food for hiking. Did you know it contains theobromine, which is good for asthma?"

Mookie snatched a bar from her hand. "Thanks!"

"You're welcome." She pulled out another bar for herself, and one for me.

"No thanks." I liked chocolate, but it wasn't worth another trip to the parallel bars.

We followed Abigail along the path, and then down the side of a steep hill lined with fir trees and something that might have been maples or oaks. I'm not all that good at trees.

"Are you totally sure about this?" I asked Abigail as we headed up the next hill.

"I'm sure. A solution isn't like a piece of clothing."

"Yeah, yeah. I know. You can't always find one that fits the way you want."

Abigail nodded. "Exactly."

We must have walked for almost an hour. Abigail and Mookie talked the whole time, but not really to each other.

Abigail pointed overhead. "Look—a red-tailed hawk."

"I wanted a Mohawk this summer," Mookie said. "Dad told me he'd give me one, but Mom said we shouldn't steal other people's cultures. Whatever that means."

"Those ferns are amazing."

"I don't like ferns. Fern Westmire punched me in the nose in second grade."

"That rock formation was probably deposited here during the last glacial period."

"Got any more chocolate?"

I just followed along behind them. I wasn't feeling very chatty. And I was worried about my thumb. I think I'd messed it up, or maybe even broken it. I could still move it, but it flopped around. And the bone looked like it was trying to poke through the skin. As much as it creeped me out, I couldn't help wiggling it like a loose tooth.

"Isn't this beautiful," Abigail said when we reached the top of another of the endless hills we'd climbed. "It's my favorite place to come when I want to do some real thinking. Look at that view. It's breathtaking."

"And the mushroom?" I asked.

Abigail pointed to a fallen tree. "There's a good place to start." She walked over and peered under the trunk. "I think I see one. Yeah. Got it!"

"Is that the last ingredient?" I asked.

"I hope so." Abigail headed back down the hill.

Not as much as I do. As great as it felt to win field day, I was ready to get back to my wheezy, unathletic existence as a living kid who could stuff his face with chicken wings and sleep late on weekends.

Abigail's mom was waiting for us when we reached

the parking lot. "Did you kids have a nice hike?" she asked.

"It was great," Abigail said. "We went all the way to the overlook. We saw a hawk, a groundhog, and five different varieties of moss."

"And look what I saw," Abigail's mom said. She pointed to a box on the front seat. "I know you and your friends like science."

I read the cover: LITTLE GENIUS CHEMISTRY SET. It showed a smiling kid holding a test tube with a mushroom cloud coming out of the top.

"Thanks, Mom." Abigail picked it up, then said, "Ohmygosh. This is dangerous. It has mercury and cadmium. And radium! They shouldn't give that to kids."

"They wouldn't sell it if it wasn't safe," her mom said.

Abigail slid the box under the seat. I had a feeling it would stay there. I wedged into the back of the van with Mookie. My feet were tired from the walk. I was glad I could feel them, but I was worried about how little of me was still alive. I stared at my thumb. Is this all I had to look forward to? Would I slowly break apart? I hoped Abigail wasn't wrong about the cure.

"I'll see you tomorrow morning," I said when we reached my house.

"Absolutely," Abigail said.

"You won't be there," her mom said. "You have a dentist appointment."

"It's just a checkup. Can't I skip it?" Abigail asked.

"Not with your sweet tooth," her mom said.

Abigail sighed and unwrapped a chocolate bar. "I'll see you guys at lunch."

Mookie got off at my house. "You know," he said as we headed inside, "my dad is always telling me how important it is to plan ahead. Mostly, I guess, because he always forgets to. Maybe you should think about stuff you could do if this cure thing doesn't happen."

"I'd rather not." I'd already spent the whole van ride thinking about how awful my life would be if I had to stay half dead.

That didn't stop Mookie. "You could do all kinds of things. Hey—you could be a food taster for a king, because poison wouldn't hurt you. How awesome is that?"

"And how would I know if the food was poison?" I asked.

"You'd . . ." Mookie scratched his head. When that didn't produce an answer, he scratched his butt. Still nothing. "Okay, maybe not a food taster. But you could be a bodyguard. Nobody can hurt you."

"I don't think bodyguards are supposed to be breakable." I wiggled my thumb again and imagined trying to tackle someone who was running at me with a gun. I could almost hear my shoulder snapping.

"Wait, I know! You could get a job as an actor in zombie movies." He held his arms out and shuffled a couple steps. "You wouldn't even need makeup. How's that for a great idea?"

"Perfect," I said. "Just perfect."

"And maybe you could make extra money as a food taster for the real actors."

I didn't bother to answer. When we got to my room, Mookie said, "Let's play checkers."

"How about something else?" Every time we played checkers, we seemed to make exactly the same moves. It got kind of boring.

"Please. I love checkers. It's the only game where I don't have trouble telling the pieces apart."

I realized Mookie had stuck by me all this time, and he hadn't asked for anything. The least I could do was play what he wanted. "Sure. I just have to find the board."

I looked under my bed and all through my bookshelves. No luck. Then I looked through my closet. That was a pain, since Mom had crammed a bunch of my stuff in these big plastic bins that were pretty hard to lift.

"Let's do something else." I was tired of lifting boxes and sorting through stuff.

"How about crazy eights?" Mookie asked. "Or war?"

"Sure." I grabbed the deck of cards from my desk. That is, I tried to. It fell right out of my hand. "Oh, no . . ."

"What's wrong?" Mookie asked.

"I lost my thumb."

"Is this some sort of weird thing like 'got your nose'?"

"No. I'm serious." I held out my right hand to show him. "My thumb is gone. I think it got sort of broken when I was twisting around on the chin-up bar. It must have snapped off or gotten snagged somewhere when I was lifting stuff." If anything could have made my stomach feel sick, this would have been it. I didn't want to look at the spot where my thumb had been.

"Isn't that what makes us human?" Mookie said. "I think that's what I heard. We have thumbs, but kangaroos don't. That's why we can build cars and make bombs and stuff, and kangaroos can't. So I guess you're only half human now."

"Knock it off. Just help me find it."

We started to search my room.

"Found it!" Mookie cried from under my bed.

As I rushed over, he said, "No, wait. My mistake. It's just an old piece of hot dog." He held it out. "But if we can't find your real thumb, maybe we can—"

"Just keep looking!" I slid open my screen. Then I grabbed the piece of hot dog from Mookie and threw it out the window. A couple seconds later, the neighbor's dalmatian, Spanky, raced across the driveway onto our lawn and gobbled up the treat. I watched for a moment to make sure he didn't keel over. He just licked his muzzle and trotted away.

I went back to searching and finally spotted my thumb

wedged between two of the large boxes in my closet. I held it in place against my hand, but it wouldn't stay. My life just kept getting worse and worse.

I was still holding the thumb when it moved. I screamed and dropped it.

"What's wrong?" Mookie asked.

I made a fist with my right hand and pretended to flex my thumb. On the floor, my thumb curled. I straightened it. Then I bent it again. I could still move it, even though it wasn't attached to me. "This is too freaky," I said.

"Hey, I've been watching you walk around for the last couple days without a heartbeat. Compared to that, this is nothing."

As I flexed and straightened my thumb, it moved across the floor like an inchworm. I crawled it to my door, and then back over to me.

"That is so cool," Mookie said. "You've got a wireless thumb."

"I guess it's good it still works." I picked it up and tried not to flex it while I was holding it.

"All you have to do is glue it back on," Mookie said.

"You think?"

"Yeah. I'm pretty sure you don't want to sew it on."

"No way." I pictured my body held together with stitches. It wouldn't hurt, but the thought creeped me out. I'd be like some kind of walking rag doll. "I don't know if glue is enough." I thought about my dead flesh.

x

107

Then I thought about that stuff my mom used for her plants. It was crazy, but I guess it was worth a try.

"Come on. I have an idea." I headed for the garage. I found a pile of small foil packets on my mom's plant-supply shelf. "This is rooting powder," I told Mookie. "My mom uses it when she want to plant something. You can take a piece of a plant stem, and this will make it grow roots." I figured, right now, I was more like a plant than a person, anyhow.

"What about the glue?"

"We have lots of that." I looked on the shelves at all the different types, then picked up a small bottle of Elmer's. "I think it has milk in it. Can't hurt."

"Yeah. Milk's good for bones."

I unscrewed the top of the glue and poured in the powder. Then I mixed it with a long screwdriver. "Let's go outside. The light's better." I didn't want to end up with my thumb glued on all crooked. When we got to the driveway, I put some of the glue on the end of my thumb and pressed it in place.

"Yeeooowwwww!"

I was definitely wrong about the "can't hurt" part. A searing pain shot through my thumb like I'd just used it to plug a leak in a volcano.

In the middle of my third or fourth scream, I noticed the pain had stopped. I pressed my thumb against my hand for a while longer, so the glue could set. Then I flexed it to make sure it still worked.

"We did it!" I said.

"High five!" Mookie said. He lifted his hand.

"High five!" I yelled, giving his hand a hard slap. I yelled something else as I watched my thumb sail through the air.

As I chased after it, I heard Spanky barking. He shot past me. I put on a burst of speed and dived for my thumb. I got there just ahead of him. As I grabbed the thumb, he clamped his teeth down on the back of my hand. An instant later, he whined and ran away. I guess I tasted worse than a piece of mummified hot dog.

"Maybe let it dry a bit longer," Mookie said as I put more glue on the end.

The pain was just as awful this time, but at least I was expecting it. I hoped I didn't break off any more pieces.

I waited until I was sure the glue had set, and then finally flexed my thumb. It bent just fine. I pressed on it gently. It seemed to hold. I gave it a little twist. No problem.

"Better?" Mookie asked.

"Yeah. It's good."

"All right. High five! Oops—never mind."

13

Star Athlete

peedy!"

"Flash!"

"SuperNathan!"

"Iron Arms Abercrombie!"

It started the moment I got to school. Everyone was thrilled about our field day win and the promise of pizza from Mr. Lomux. Mookie stuck as close to me as he could, trying to soak up some of the glory.

"I'm his trainer," he said to every kid who came near us. "We're going to get a sneaker deal." Nobody paid any attention to him. He didn't seem to mind.

In a way, the small slice of glory was nice, though this

wasn't the best time in my life to be getting noticed. I was looking a lot paler than usual, and I had to try to remember to blink once in a while so I wouldn't creep people out. But it was definitely a new experience for me to be any sort of star athlete. I figured I should try to enjoy it, since it wasn't going to last.

Kids waved at me from a couple different tables when I went into the cafeteria. But I took my tray right to the Table of the Doomed. I needed to talk with Abigail, and I really didn't care where I sat. The dead zone on my legs had almost reached my ankles. There wasn't a whole lot of living meat between me and permanent zombiehood. I didn't want to spend the rest of my life—I mean, my death—gluing pieces back on.

"Got it?" I asked.

Before Abigail could answer, Mookie said, "Uh-oh. Intruder alert." He pointed at Shawna, who was heading right for us.

"I wonder what she wants," Abigail muttered.

"It can't be good," Mookie said.

"I'm having a Halloween party tomorrow night, Nathan," Shawna said.

Good grief. Did she forget that she'd already pulled that joke on me? I guess she didn't bother keeping track of her victims. I thought about ignoring her, but even that would give her too much satisfaction when she told me I wasn't invited. So I beat her to it. "I know. I'm not invited. Ha, ha. Now go away."

111

Shawna frowned like I'd just spoken to her in Portuguese. "Of course you're invited. All the cool kids are coming." She held out an envelope. My first name was written on it with very curly letters. When I didn't take the envelope, she placed it on the table and walked away.

I watched out of the corner of my eyes as she left. The girls at her table whispered and giggled, but it didn't sound like mocking laughter. I stared down at the envelope. "Probably some sort of cruel joke."

"I'll see." Mookie flipped the envelope over with his fork, then held it down and slipped his knife under the flap, smearing the envelope with brown gravy from his turkey sandwich.

"Why are you doing that?" I asked.

"There might be a bomb," he said.

"And how exactly is silverware going to save us?" Abigail asked.

Mookie ignored her and cut open the envelope, revealing an invitation. "Cool. Look at this. She's having games and a DJ." Mookie started reading all the stuff on the invitation. "Six-foot sandwiches! Wow. I wonder if each guest gets one?"

"I think it's one or two sandwiches for the whole party," I said.

Abigail leaned over and looked at the invitation. "She's going to have a chocolate fountain!"

"What's that?" Mookie asked.

"It's a fountain with melted chocolate," she said. "You dip fruit in it."

"Forget the fruit," Mookie said. "I'd swim in it."

"Chocolate is actually good for your skin," Abigail said.

"You're so lucky, Nate," Mookie said. "I wish I was going."

"I'm not lucky," I said. "And I'm not going to her party. She only invited me because I won field day. My body might be different. But inside, I'm the same person she was mean to last week."

I picked up the invitation and walked over to Shawna's table. All the way there, I imagined what I'd tell her. *You're spoiled rotten.* No, that was me. *You're mean and cruel.* Yeah. That was true. But if I called her names, wasn't I being mean and cruel?

I decided to keep it simple. I dropped the invitation in front of her and said, "Sorry. I can't make it."

I didn't even bother to wait for her reaction. It was reward enough for me to know I'd shocked her.

"What did you do?" Abigail asked when I got back.

"I told her I didn't want to go. Forget about that. Is the cure ready?"

Abigail stared up at the ceiling and tugged at the end of her hair for a moment, as if thinking about a whole lot of stuff at once. It must be tough being so smart. "Almost."

"Almost?" I put my foot on my chair, pulled up my

pants cuff, and pushed down my sock. "I'm down to here," I said, pointing to the spot above my ankle where life and death met. "That's all I've got left."

"Trust me. I won't let you down. There's just one element remaining. I'm positive. Based on my calculations, you're not in danger until late Friday night. You've got a day and a half."

"I'm already in danger in other ways." I told her about my thumb, and about the rooting powder. "How could it move by itself?"

"The same way you can move. I believe the answer is buried in the deepest mysteries of physics and biology. It might even involve quantum mechanics." Abigail spread her hands and smiled. "Or magic."

I had a more important question for her. "Why do you think it hurt?"

"I'm not sure." Abigail looked up at the ceiling again. I guess all the answers in the universe were written there in some kind of ink that was visible only to really smart people. "Maybe the nerves came back to life, but just for a moment. The zombie part of you took right back over. But the cure will fix that."

I thought about my whole body getting flooded with the same sort of pain I'd felt in my thumb. "Will the cure hurt?"

"Probably not. Look—stop worrying and trust me. Okay?"

"I'll try." I had no choice. I had to trust her. But the

rest of the day went by in a blur. I couldn't concentrate on anything. I just kept picturing what my life would be like if I didn't get cured. I don't think Mr. Lomux would be very impressed with my athletic abilities if my hand went flying off when I served a volleyball or I lost a leg on the pommel horse.

I guess Mookie knew what I was thinking. At the end of the day, he said, "Cheer up. Maybe you didn't like my other ideas, but I thought of something even cooler. You could go around the country giving chin-up demonstrations. Hey—I'll bet that's what people mean when they say, 'Keep your chin up.'"

My head slumped, chin and all.

I did like one of Mookie's ideas, and it was still working for me. I had no trouble at dinner as I pushed pieces of roast beef under my mashed potatoes. But later that evening, I noticed Mom kept watching me every time I walked through the living room.

I sneaked a glance at my reflection in the window. There was nothing about me that was obviously screaming *Zombie!*

"Are you feeling okay?" she asked.

"Yeah. I feel great. Why?"

"Usually, you go to the bathroom either right after school or about an hour and a half after dinner."

"Mom!" I couldn't believe she paid that much attention to the personal details of my life.

"It's a mother's job to notice this sort of thing. I'm

pretty sure you haven't been going to the bathroom the last couple days. Are you constipated?"

"No! I'm at school most of the day," I said. "They have lots of bathrooms there. I'm fine. Honest. Can we drop the subject?"

"Just tell me if you need help. There are some very gentle laxatives."

"I will." I got out of the living room as fast as I could. But I made sure to go into the bathroom half an hour later.

"It's a good thing I'm getting cured tomorrow," I muttered as I sat and waited for enough time to pass. When I came out, Mom smiled at me like I'd just brought home straight A's.

That night, I beat four different online games before 3 A.M. I decided to look for something different to do. Some of the kids in school talked a lot about these multi-player games, where you went into a whole world filled with people and monsters. You could have adventures, but you could also chat with other players. I found a free one, downloaded it, and signed up.

That kept me busy until it was time to sneak off to bed and pretend to be asleep. I remembered the lesson from last night. When Mom woke me, I dashed right for the bathroom. It wasn't hard for me to leap out of bed like I was in a rush. I didn't need to go to the bathroom, but I was really eager to get to school. This was the day I'd finally come back to life.

14

On Second Thought

Instead of meeting up with Mookie on Friday morning, I ran past the school, all the way to Abigail's house, and banged on the door.

"Why, you're Abigail's little friend," her mom said. "Come in. Abigail will be right down."

I stepped inside. It wasn't easy. The entryway was lined with boxes and stacks of newspapers. The hall past Mrs. Goldberg was filled with more boxes, magazines, and small appliances.

"Nathan?" Abigail jogged down the stairs.

"I wanted to talk about our science project," I said.

"Of course." Abigail nodded, got a kiss from her mom, and slipped outside.

"The cure?" I asked as we walked off the porch.

"We're in great shape," she said. "I know the last ingredient. We need alexandrite."

"What's that?"

"It's a rare gem. It's purple."

"A gem?" I felt like I was playing a high-stakes game of animal, vegetable, or mineral. "Where are we going to find that?"

"Shawna has one. She wears this charm bracelet sometimes. I saw it on her wrist last week. There's a tiny chip of alexandrite on one of the charms."

I stopped to let all of this sink in. "So you're telling me I have to steal a bracelet?"

Abigail shook her head. "No, we don't have to steal it. Just borrow it for a minute. It will help speed up the reaction between the fish scales and the mushroom. But it won't be ruined or anything. It's called a catalyst."

"There's no way she's going to let us borrow it."

"I know. But we don't have to ask her. All you have to do is get us into Shawna's house."

"Us?"

"You'll need Mookie and me to help. We might have to create a distraction. We've already seen how good he is at that."

"I guess I'd better find out if I can still get invited." I think there was a part of me that wanted to hang out with the cool kids. Of course, there was also only a very small part of me that was still alive.

We headed for school. Abigail scurried to catch up with me. "I never walked to school with anyone before," she said.

"It's not as exciting as it sounds."

As we walked, I wiggled my left little finger, which was feeling a bit loose. At least my thumb seemed to be holding on solidly. I'd started carrying a small bottle of the special glue mixture with me, just in case I needed to stick some other body part back on.

As we were crossing the street, Abigail said, "Go ahead. You're dying to ask."

"About what?"

"The boxes. The clutter. You must be curious."

"It's none of my business."

"But you're curious, right?"

"Right." I had to admit I wondered what was going on.

"Mom's always collected stuff. But it got a lot worse after Dad died." As she reached the end of that sentence, Abigail gulped like she'd swallowed something too large for her throat.

After Dad died.

The words seemed to wrap around her like a heavy cloth. I didn't look at her while I waited for her to go on. We were almost at the school when she spoke again.

"He could always talk her into getting rid of some of it. We were renting a place back then. After he was gone, the apartment got so full of Mom's stuff, they asked us to leave. That was fine. It was good for us to get away from there. Dad had left us enough money to buy a house."

I thought about my room. And Mookie's room. "I've seen worse," I said.

"Thanks."

The silence came back. I had to say something. "That must be really hard, losing your dad." I wondered whether it was especially painful for her to be around someone who was dead but still walking.

"Yeah. It's been tough. But I guess it feels good to talk about it. I've been sort of keeping it to myself."

I think I finally understood why Abigail wanted to come up with a formula to erase hurt feelings. She'd been carrying around this big hurt, and she'd never had any real friends to share it with. Too bad the formula hadn't worked out.

When we reached the school, I saw Shawna and her friends near the flagpole. "Wish me luck." I jogged toward them, trying to look like a track star.

"Nathan, wait," Abigail called after me.

"Hang on. I'll be right back," I shouted over my shoulder. I wanted to get this over with. I got ready to beg Shawna to let me go to her party.

"Hi, Nathan," she said. "Are you sure you can't come to my party?"

"I'll come!" I hadn't meant to shout. I hoped the next

part would be just as easy. "Is it okay if I bring a couple friends?"

"That would be great. I'm sure your friends are just as cool as you are." She flashed me one of her dazzling smiles, and for a billionth of a second, I almost believed I was a cool guy with cool friends.

"Thanks." I rushed off to tell Abigail the news. By the time I got there, Mookie had joined her.

"We're going," I said. "What did you want to tell me?"

Her gaze flickered over toward Shawna, and then back to me. "It's not important."

"You sure?"

"Yeah. Forget about it." She turned toward Mookie. "Ready for a party?"

"You bet," Mookie said. "I'm a total party animal."

"So, what's our plan?" I asked.

"We'll find out where she keeps the bracelet," Abigail said. "If necessary, Mookie will cause an initial distraction."

"I can stick my face in the chocolate fountain and blow bubbles," he said.

"That might be a bit extreme," Abigail said. "Either way, once she's distracted, I'll sneak off, get the bracelet, and use the stone as the catalyst."

"I hope this works," I said.

"It will," Abigail said. "I guarantee it will."

I looked across the school yard and noticed that Rodney was glaring at me again.

"You go ahead," I told Mookie and Abigail. "I'll be there in a minute." I wasn't going to spend the whole day trying to avoid Rodney. I waited for him to walk over.

He poked me in the chest. "If you go to Shawna's party, I'm going to hurt you."

I was sick of his bullying. I curled my hands into fists. "You can't hurt me." True. But then I looked down and saw my left little finger dangling. I might not feel pain, and I might be able to hurt Rodney, but I didn't want him pounding on my face hard enough to knock pieces off, even if I did have my glue with me. I stared at him, hoping he'd decided not to start a fight on school property.

He stared back for a moment. "Now you're really asking for it. If you go to the party, you're leaving in pieces." He gave me a hard shove, then walked away.

That was close. I really didn't want to have to glue my jaw back on. But I'd stood up to him. And that felt good. I thought about all the bad stuff I'd gone through last week—the party, gym class, the video game. I realized there was something I had to do before Abigail brought me back to life. At lunchtime, I walked over to Caleb at the nerd table. "Hi, vidiot," he said. But he added, "Nice job on field day."

"Thanks." I pointed to the game. "I've got one more thing I need to win."

"You really don't want to do that," he said.

"Yeah, I really do."

"It's your funeral," Caleb said.

As he was handing me the game, I said, "Set it at the hardest level."

I watched as he cycled past EASY, MEDIUM, HARD, and KILLER all the way to UNBEATABLE.

"This won't take long," he said.

"No. It won't."

His smirk faded as my first guy blasted through wave after wave of zombies. I felt kids crowding around me. It brought back a bad memory of the other day in art class. But memories had no effect on my steadiness. I blew through the whole first level in record time. Then I handed the game back to Caleb. "Here. That's enough. You can finish it for me."

He took the game, but didn't manage to say anything. I moved through the parting crowd of staring eyes and open mouths. Maybe for the moment, I wasn't the closest thing to a zombie in the room.

The rest of the school day passed without making much of an impression on me. I guess this must be what it's like for the class gerbil. Or maybe gerbils had deep thoughts. I sure didn't.

I killed time in my room by reading until it was late enough to head out for the party. I still needed a costume. Halloween was actually tomorrow. I guess Shawna had her party on Friday so everyone could go out for candy on Saturday. I liked going out, but I never made a big deal about dressing up. I usually just threw something together at the last minute.

I really didn't care all that much what I looked like. I wasn't going there to make friends. I was going there to steal—okay, borrow—jewelry and escape from my existence as one of the walking dead. A pirate costume seemed about right for that. I got a large bandanna from Mom and tied it on my head. I also got a large round clip-on earring. Arrrgghhh.

Before I left, I grabbed a pin and checked my legs. At first, when I couldn't find any feeling, I started to panic. The tops and sides of my feet were dead. The only life left was in small circles on the bottoms of my feet.

I met Mookie and Abigail at the corner FoodMart a couple blocks from Shawna's house. Abigail was wearing a rumpled white shirt, along with a white wig and a white mustache.

"I'm Albert Einstein," she said before I could ask. "I'm the schmartest theoretical physicist in the universe."

Mookie's face was covered with hair.

"I'm a werewolf," he said.

"That's a weird mask," I told him.

"It's not a mask," he said. "I got some hair and glued it on. It took all afternoon. I used really strong glue, so it will still be on tomorrow night when we go out for trick or treat."

I looked closer and realized the hairs were all sorts of different colors. "Where'd you get it?"

"Behind the barbershop," he said. "They throw out tons of hair, if you ever need any."

"I'll keep that in mind." I turned to little Einstein. "Do you have the ingredients with you so you can use the gem?"

"Right here." Abigail lifted her purse. "How are you doing with the deadline?"

I touched my index finger to my thumb, making a small circle. "Just the bottom of my foot."

"That's all we need. As long as there's even a tiny patch of living body, the cure will work. By the way, my mom had to go out, but she said you guys could come over. She made some of her famous Crock-Pot chili. We can all go to my house after the party and celebrate your ability to eat again. I suspect you'll be starving."

"Chili!" Mookie said. "I love chili. It gives me gas, but I don't care."

"Everything gives you gas," I said.

As we got closer to Shawna's house, I could hear music blasting. "This will be great," Mookie said.

"It will be fascinating to observe," Abigail said. "I've always wondered what happens at a party."

"You've never been to one?" Mookie asked.

"I've never wanted to go to one," she said. "I had lots of chances. I was just never interested."

I knocked on the door. Shawna answered it, wearing a princess costume. For a fraction of a second, I almost felt my heart beat. To say she looked pretty would be sort of like saying the Eiffel Tower looked tall.

"Hi, Nathan!" Shawna smiled at me. I blinked my eyes to keep them from popping out. Then her expression changed. She pointed at Abigail and Mookie. "What are those two losers doing here?"

15

▼

Disinvited

Mookie's face flushed. His eyes and mouth widened into perfect circles, making him look like a hairy bowling ball. Abigail shuddered like she'd been smacked between the shoulder blades with a telephone pole. I froze. I didn't have a clue what to do.

"But you told me . . ." I searched for a way to get them inside.

Then Abigail sprang into action. She slapped herself in the forehead. Then she grabbed Mookie's arm, and said, "Oops. This is the wrong house. My mistake. Come on."

She dragged Mookie down the steps. When I caught her eye, she made a shooing motion with the back of her hand, like she wanted me to go in by myself. Then she pointed to the sidewalk. I guess she and Mookie were going to wait for me out there. It was up to me to get the bracelet.

The good news was, I already knew where to find the bracelet. The bad news was that it was on Shawna's wrist. Oh boy.

"Well, don't just stand there. Come in," Shawna said. She looked toward the sidewalk and muttered, "Stupid losers."

I wanted to shout at her and stomp away. If anything else had been at stake, I would have told her that she was the loser, and didn't deserve to have kids as cool as Mookie and Abigail at her party. But my whole future was at stake. I stole another glance at my friends, then followed Shawna inside.

So there I was, surrounded by everything that was on the invitation. A DJ was playing music in one corner. The chocolate fountain, surrounded by cut fruit, bubbled and flowed in another corner. Between the DJ and the fountain, two six-foot sandwiches, one of which was now about a yard short, sat on a table along the wall, next to another table full of cups, soda bottles, and pitchers of punch.

"Hey, Nathan." Mort, dressed as a mummy, pointed one of his crutches at me. The Decker twins waved at me from the snack table and shouted, "Aaarrrghhh!" They were both wearing Captain Hook costumes. I guess this was the year for pirates. And I guess neither of them wanted to be Peter Pan.

I was surrounded by the cool kids. A couple were dancing. Most were just sitting around, talking. It was nice. But I wasn't there for partying. I was there for alexandrite. The charm bracelet dangled from Shawna's wrist. One of the charms definitely had a tiny gem on it. *Maybe it will fall off*, I thought.

Yeah, and maybe I'd learn to fly by flapping my ears. The only way I was going to get what I needed was to take it myself. I might not have much time. Rodney was there, dressed like a zombie in torn clothes and badly done makeup. Someone who's that ugly when he's alive really shouldn't try to look dead. He was carrying a bloody rubber hand. I watched as he walked up to Lexi and thrust it in her face.

She shrieked and jumped back, then giggled. Rodney growled, limped toward Cydnie, and thrust the hand at her with pretty much the same results. Then he chewed on it. It looked like he was working up the nerve to approach Shawna. But as he staggered toward Bekkah, Shawna dashed over, grabbed the hand from him, and threw it across the room. "Stop that," she said. "It's not very funny."

Rodney let out a weak growl. I guess he was trying to be cute. It didn't work. Shawna turned away from him.

That's when he caught sight of me. He shot me a glare and pounded his fist into his palm. I was getting sick of his threats. But he wasn't my biggest problem. Right now, I needed to figure out how to get the alexandrite.

I really wished I had Abigail and Mookie there to help me snatch the bracelet. Abigail would be able to invent a brilliant plan involving science or logic. Mookie would dream up something so crazy that it might actually work. I looked out the window. They were on the sidewalk, standing near a low brick wall that ran along the front edge of the lawn.

What would they do if they were here? Mookie would probably scream, "Killer bracelet! Save her!" and pluck it right off her wrist. Abigail would trick her out of it with some kind of brilliant argument. Or she'd whip out a laser and heat the bracelet up from across the room. I needed to do something fast, or Rodney might try to make good on his promise that I'd leave the party in pieces. He'd already started to move toward me.

Pieces . . .

"Got it!" I gasped as the idea hit me. I didn't know if it was brilliant or crazy, but it was all I had. In a weird way, I had Rodney to thank for it. I walked over to Shawna and said, "You look thirsty. Let me get you a drink." I made sure I spoke loudly enough for Rodney to hear me, too.

"Thanks. That's very sweet of you, Nathan." Her voice was sparkly now—totally different from the one she'd used to call my friends losers. If Rodney was a slug crossed with a gorilla, I guess Shawna was a chameleon crossed with a cobra.

At the snack table, I poured a glass full of orange soda, did something awful I really didn't want to think about, and then headed back toward Shawna. I was ready to give her the drink myself, if I had to, but I really hoped I'd just suckered Rodney into doing the dirty work for me, because Shawna was going to totally hate whoever handed her that cup. And if anyone deserved to be hated, it was Rodney.

"I'll take that," Rodney said, grabbing my shoulder.

I paused for a second, like I was thinking about arguing. If I gave up too easily, he might get suspicious. I think he dug his fingers deeper into my shoulder, but it was hard to tell since there wasn't any pain. I moaned like a wimp and handed him the cup. His evil smirk erased any guilt I felt over what was about to happen to him. Like a dog taking a ball back to his owner, Rodney carried the soda to Shawna.

Please work, please work, please work. . . .

Shawna raised the cup to her lips and took a sip.

Notice it, notice it, notice it. . . .

She took a second sip. I wiggled my fingers slightly.

Right now, right now, right now . . .

Shawna frowned and tilted the cup. She froze. Her eyes grew wider. And wider. I got ready to spring into action.

A moment later, the scream erupted. Shawna flung the cup from her, spraying orange soda all over the room.

I saw two things beside the cup and soda fly through the air. I needed both of them. Luckily, they went in roughly the same direction. Even more luckily, they didn't fly toward the chocolate fountain. I followed the trail of soda-splashed kids and then dived to the floor.

I found the bracelet first. It was under the couch. I had to search a bit longer for my little finger. I definitely hadn't enjoyed tearing it off. There wasn't any pain, but it was still the single most awful thing I'd ever done. Once I was cured and sleeping again, I'd probably have a lifetime of nightmares about this.

Part of me felt bad for Shawna. Even if she was mean and cruel, she didn't really deserve to find a finger in her soda. As for Rodney, I'm glad I'd tricked him into handing the glass to her. I hoped this would mess up his dating plans. After I found my finger, I headed out the door and raced over to Mookie and Abigail. Just like Rodney said, I was leaving there in pieces. Nobody paid any attention when I left. Shawna's scream had set off a spreading panic.

"Got it," I said as I held up the bracelet. "Let's finish the cure."

"We can do it at my house," Abigail said. "There's time."

Something caught my eye. I moved under a streetlight. Alexandrite was sort of purple. Abigail had told me that. And, after she mentioned it, I'd looked it up online to see if there was another way to get some. Close up, I could see that the stone in the charm was red. I checked all the other charms. There weren't any other stones.

Oh, no . . . I'd stolen the wrong bracelet. It never even occurred to me that Shawna might have more than one charm bracelet. Of all the stupid, idiotic moves I could make, I'd managed to do the one thing that would absolutely doom me. "This isn't alexandrite. . . ." I felt like all my hopes had just been smashed with a gigantic sledgehammer.

"No. It looks like a ruby," Abigail said.

I stomped my foot on the sidewalk to see if there was any life left in it. A tiny spot, no larger than a dime, stung. The rest was dead. I was almost out of time.

16

▼

Taking the Cure

I **can't believe** I messed up. It's over. I'll be dead forever." My chest jerked like I was having the biggest asthma attack of my life. I expected my lungs to cry for air. But they didn't need it. They'd never need it again. My brain went into overdrive. I fell to my knees. "I'm dead. I'm really dead." I couldn't stop saying it. The cry morphed into a single howl pouring from my throat.

"Nathan, it's okay." Abigail tugged at my arm. "Come with me."

"Why? What's the point? I'm dead. Just leave me alone."

Mookie leaned over and slapped my face. It didn't hurt, but it got my attention. "What was that for?"

"You're hysterical," he said. "You're supposed to slap people when they get like that."

I reached up and slapped him back. He staggered away, clutching at his cheek. I stood, mindless and angry, and headed toward him for another slap. I snarled a wordless growl.

"Nathan!" Abigail shouted. "Stop it." She dragged me over to the brick wall. "Sit down. And take off your shoe. We don't need the gem."

"What? I don't understand."

Her voice got very quiet. "The scales and the mushroom are really all we needed."

"What do you mean?" I stared at her, but she didn't meet my eye.

"It was a lie," she said.

"Why?" Mookie asked.

I realized I knew the answer. "You wanted to go to the party."

Abigail nodded.

"There's nothing wrong with that," Mookie said. "I wanted to go to the party. I still do."

"We all wanted to go," I said. As much as Abigail acted like it wasn't important, I knew she was just like me, and like all the kids who weren't at the coolest table and didn't get to go to the coolest parties—or any parties. We all pretended we didn't care. But we all wanted a chance to find out how it felt to be on the other side of the window.

Abigail whispered something I couldn't make out.

"What did you say?"

"I made up the part about the mushroom, too."

"Why?"

"It was so much fun when we went to the aquarium for the fish scale. Wasn't it?"

"Yeah," Mookie said. "That's the best place I've ever been kicked out of."

"At first, you were just a test subject," Abigail said. "I needed to observe the Hurt-Be-Gone before I used it on myself. Then I got to know you. It was so cool hanging out with you and Mookie. I never had friends before. I always pretended I didn't need them. When I was little, none of the other kids understood me. They made fun of me. So I stopped trying to make friends. But you guys are so cool. You don't mind that I'm smart, and you never make fun of me. I wanted to do more stuff with you. You're the best."

"So you dragged us through the woods?" I asked. "And you tricked me into going to the party."

Her head drooped lower. "I wanted to go. But I wasn't being selfish. And least, not totally. I wanted it for you and Mookie, too. I wanted you to be popular. Everyone would like you if they really got to know you."

"That's true," Mookie said. "I know us, and I like us."

"It doesn't work that way," I said. "We'll never be

popular." But even as I spoke, I realized it wasn't that simple, or that hopeless. Some of the kids at the party, and at school, seemed to like me for myself, and not just because of field day. I'd actually started to like Abigail once I got to know her. And I'd stopped liking Shawna at all when I got to know what she was really like.

Abigail's head snapped up. "Listen, I was wrong. I'll admit it. I used you. And I lied to you. But we need to apply the cure now. Immediately. You can yell at me later. I guess I deserve it." Abigail reached in her purse and pulled out a plastic butter container.

She lifted the lid and took out a Band-Aid. The wrapper was off, but the paper was still covering the strips. As she bent back the paper, I saw a blob of rainbow-colored jelly quiver on the pad.

"Is that it?" I asked.

"Yeah. I made the cure from the scales. It really did take a long time to extract the ingredients. I didn't lie about that part. But it's ready now. That's all that matters. Come on—you need to wear it on the live part of you. Take off your shoe."

I slipped off my shoe and pulled off my sock. Abigail stuck the Band-Aid on the bottom of my foot. I gritted my teeth, but there wasn't any pain. A warm tingle spread outward from the spot. The warmth crawled across the bottom of my foot and seeped toward my ankles. It was the nicest thing I'd ever felt.

"I think it's working," I whispered.

"You'll feel normal in an hour or two."

"And that's it? I'll be alive again?"

"Yes. But listen carefully," Abigail said as I pulled my sock back on. "You have to wear this until you are completely cured. You have to let it spread to every inch of your body, all the way to the top of your head. Do you understand? You need to leave it on until you are completely normal."

"Then I guess it's never coming off," Mookie said.

Abigail spun toward him. "This isn't a joke!" Then she looked back at me. "Do you understand?"

"Sure. If I take it off before I'm cured, I'm in big trouble."

"Right. And it won't happen slowly. It will be like a stretched rubber band snapping back. You'll be all zombie, forever."

"No way I'd let that happen," I said.

My nightmare was almost over. I was about to rejoin the living, breathing, pain-feeling, inhaler-sucking world. I'd miss the ability to swim underwater or play video games like an expert, but it was stuff I'd happily give up in exchange for the chance to burn my mouth on hot pizza or shiver in a rainstorm.

"Uh-oh." I reached in my pocket and grabbed my little finger and the bottle of glue. "I'd better stick this on while my hand is still dead."

It hurt just as much as I remembered. My scream of pain was matched by a shout from behind us.

"And don't ever come back!"

Rodney was getting kicked out of Shawna's house. Loudly. As he walked down the steps, Shawna followed him, yelling stuff you normally don't hear from girls when they're in public.

"You lousy stinking evil creepy guy. You slime-sucking brainless prank-playing dirtwad. You heap of warmed-over snot clumps."

It got worse. Shawna yelled at Rodney all the way to the end of her lawn. He slumped down like a dog that had just been punished for ripping up a sofa cushion. Then she yelled at him all the way to the corner. I had to admit she had an impressive vocabulary.

"Here." I handed her the bracelet when she came back. "I think you dropped this."

She took the bracelet from me, but she seemed like she was sort of in a fog. I guess the horror of almost swallowing my little finger had been pretty hard on her. "Nathan. Why are you leaving? The party just started."

"Because I don't want to ditch my friends."

"So come on in. All of you."

"Sure. That would be great." It was nice that everyone would finally get to join the party.

"Yes!" Mookie said.

"No thanks," Abigail said.

"No?" Mookie looked rapidly back and forth from me to Abigail, then squeezed his eyes shut and yelled,

"You guys decide! I can't handle the pressure." With all the hair on his face, he looked like a coconut.

"We'll be right there," I told Shawna.

"Great." She headed back in.

"What's that about?" I asked Abigail. "You're dying to go in there."

"Not anymore. I was being foolish."

"No, you weren't," I said. "There's nothing wrong with wanting to be popular. And there's nothing wrong with most of the kids in there. Actually, most of them are pretty nice."

"I don't care. I'm going home and having chili. You can come if you want." Abigail walked away from us.

Mookie opened his eyes. "Ahhhhh! I don't know what to do."

"Well, come inside and think about it." I knew Abigail wanted me to chase after her. But I was tired of being a puppet. And, as thrilled as I was to be cured, I was annoyed with her for making me run all over the place, and tricking me, and letting me get so close to being dead.

"Come on, Mookie. Let's party." I headed for the steps. Mookie followed me.

A party was a weird place to be while my body was returning from death. The room vibrated with loud music and pulsed with moving, living bodies. By now, life had spread past my ankles. Soon, it would reach the top of my head, and I'd be just another normal guy.

I noticed that Shawna didn't drink any more soda. I

felt sort of sorry for her, but I think she deserved to suffer a bit for the way she'd treated my friends.

It was nice hanging out with a bunch of kids. But there was a part of me that couldn't seem to enjoy what I was doing. By the time the life had reached my chest—and my heart, I guess—I started feeling a little guilty about the way I'd ditched Abigail. She'd looked so small and lonely as she shuffled off to her pot of chili. All she'd really wanted was to find a way to deal with the one huge hurt in her life. She'd suffered a pretty big loss.

By the time the life reached my chin, I was feeling a lot more than just a little guilty. I'd be totally cured soon, and it was all because of Abigail. I could picture her sitting up in her room with a bowl of chili as she read the encyclopedia or looked at stuff through her microscope.

"Had enough?" I asked Mookie, who was staring out the window in the direction of Abigail's house.

He nodded, but wasn't able to speak, since his mouth was filled with potato chips, pretzels, and popcorn—all of which he'd dipped in chocolate.

"Maybe we should go see Abigail," I said.

I thanked Shawna for inviting me. Then Mookie and I headed out. We were two blocks away from Abigail's house when I realized my breathing was completely back. I sniffed the air and asked Mookie, "Do you smell that?"

"Why do I always get blamed when there's a smell?" he asked.

"No. Not that. I smell smoke."

He sniffed. "Yeah. Someone's got a fire going."

"I like fireplaces." I felt the top of my head. Life had returned to almost all of my body. I'd be completely cured in just a couple more minutes. This winter, I could sit by a fire, feel the warmth, and sip hot cocoa. It would be great.

We were a block away from Abigail's house when I saw the large plume of black smoke. Huge dark clouds rose in the air, blotting out the moon.

An unfamiliar feeling shot through my stomach. Panic. As we raced closer, I saw flames reaching out from the downstairs windows, licking at the walls and climbing higher.

"I'll bet it was that Crock-Pot," I said. "It must have caught fire." Abigail had said her mom wasn't home. I really hoped Abigail wasn't home, either.

We ran toward her house, shouting, "Fire!" By now, the whole place was burning like a crumpled piece of paper in a fireplace.

My hopes crumpled, too, when I saw someone at an upstairs window. Abigail was inside.

17

▼

Flame and Fortune

"Help!"

It was a faint scream, muffled by the glass. Abigail, no longer wearing the wig or mustache, was trying to get the window open. And then she collapsed.

Far off—way too far off—I heard the faint sound of sirens from the other side of the valley.

"They'll never get here in time." I raced for the door. A couple people had gathered by the middle of the lawn, but they didn't move any closer to the house. I guess the heat was holding them back.

Nothing was going to stop me. Sweat rolled off my face, but I ignored the heat. I grabbed the knob, then yelled and pulled my arm back as the hot metal seared my fingers.

I kicked at the door. The fire must have damaged it enough so it was weakened. It splintered off the hinges. I could barely make out the stairs ahead of me in the smoke-filled air. Two steps in, I had to back off. The smoke hit my lungs like a scouring pad. I couldn't breathe.

"Nathan!" Mookie yelled. "Stop! It's too dangerous."

"I have to try."

Abigail would die if I didn't save her. Die for real and forever. The smoke would kill her. I'd die if I tried to get inside. But the smoke couldn't kill me if I was already dead. There was no time to think about it. I pulled off my shoe, yanked off my sock, and ripped off the Band-Aid.

Death returned with stunning force.

I felt like I'd been thumped on top of my head by a giant fist. I fell flat on my back. My body went numb. But I no longer smelled smoke. My eyes no longer burned. My lungs stopped screaming for clean air.

I slipped my shoe back on and rushed into Abigail's house. I couldn't feel the heat anymore, but I could hear the fire. It whooshed and crackled all around me. I checked my clothes to make sure they hadn't burst into flames. I could be burning up and not even know it.

Abigail had been at a window on the left side of the house. I raced up the stairs. I couldn't see a thing. I wanted to escape. Ever since I was little, I had avoided any kind of smoke. I was sure I was going to pass out. I fought my panic and kept going.

I felt along the hallway until I reached a door. I moved straight across the room from the door until I hit the wall. Then I crawled along the baseboard until I found Abigail. She was crumpled against the wall by the window.

It would take too long to drag her out of the house. I lifted her in my arms and raced back to the stairs. It's a miracle I found my way. I couldn't see. I couldn't really feel, except for the slightest sense of pressure. But I had no choice except to get out—so that's what I did.

Fire covered the walls downstairs, but I knew I could get through quickly enough so Abigail would be okay. I just hoped she hadn't inhaled too much smoke already. She looked like she was asleep.

"Sleep isn't death," I whispered.

The instant I reached the lawn, someone grabbed Abigail from my arms and started giving her mouth-to-mouth resuscitation.

I staggered back. A living person would be exhausted, coughing, choking, and trembling. I was just scared. My arms and legs felt dead. I wiggled my toes in my shoes. They were dead. Like the rest of me.

All of me. I was a complete zombie. Forever.

Mookie came over and joined me. Before he could say anything, I heard a cough. Abigail opened her eyes.

I knelt down next to her. "You okay?"

She nodded. "You didn't—?"

I shrugged. "Yeah, I did."

"But . . ."

"A very smart person once told me, a solution isn't like a piece of clothing. You can't always find one that fits the way you want."

"I guess, sometimes, you just have to take the wedgie," Mookie said.

Abigail smiled at me and whispered. "Hi, zombie."

I returned the smile. "Hi, smartie."

Someone slapped me on the back. "You're a hero, boy!"

"It was nothing."

I stayed with Abigail until the ambulance came. They took her to the hospital to check her out. But I knew she'd be okay.

"You're a zombie," Mookie said. "Forever."

He was right. There was nothing I could do about it. No way I could change what I'd done. There was really only one thing to say. I spread my arms, shrugged, and said, "I'll live."

Later

Abigail **was fine.** Her house burned to the ground. But it was insured. So Abigail and her mom will get to live in a new house—without all the magazines, boxes, jars, and dangerous appliances. That should make her happy.

According to Abigail, her uncle Zardo somehow made his way to Bezimo Island, where he's working as a tour guide. I guess he's taking a break from science.

Rodney tried to pick a fight with me at lunch on Monday, but our whole table, which now included the Doomed, chased him out of the cafeteria. Shawna doesn't seem to have any idea who I am. That's fine with me.

The fire department insisted on throwing a party for me. They told me I could have anything I wanted. All I asked for was a chocolate fountain. Abigail was thrilled. But I had to keep grabbing Mookie to stop him from bobbing for berries.

My fame faded pretty quickly, especially since I made sure not to do anything too amazing during gym. But Mr. Lomux lets me be a captain once in a while. I always pick Mookie first. Nobody except for him is very happy about that. I don't care. Life isn't a popularity contest.

Speaking of life—the dead life is turning out to be a lot more lively than I'd expected. I've got some cool abilities, and I keep stumbling across new ones. Abigail is doing some research about it and helping me figure out ways to deal with some of the bigger problems. And Mookie has thought up plenty of totally gross stuff for me to do. You wouldn't believe some of the schemes he's come up with for us to make money.

Other than that, things are pretty much normal for the only zombie in Belgosi Upper Elementary. Or, at least, they were normal until the secret agent from BUM showed up. But that's another story.

SEE BELOW FOR A SNEAK PEEK AT

Nathan Abercrombie, Accidental Zombie
BOOK 2

1

▼

Leaf Me Alone

It's **pretty creepy** when some stranger follows you, spies on you, and tries to discover the deep, dark, disturbing secret that only your two closest friends in the world know about. It's even creepier when it happens three times in one day.

It started Monday morning when Mookie and I were walking to school. He'd stayed over because his parents were out of town all weekend. They'd won a free trip to somewhere in Vermont. Well, I guess it was sort of free. They had to pay for the bus and the hotel, but I think they got dinner or something.

"I hope they bring me maple syrup," Mookie said as we headed out the door. "It's not just for pancakes, you know. It's good on everything. Even chicken wings."

"I think I'd pick hot sauce," I said. "Not that I'll

COPYRIGHT © 2009 BY DAVID LUBAR

probably ever eat wings again." Food didn't play a big part in my life—or death—these days.

"Hey, there's no law that says you have to stick with one sauce. You can combine them. Chocolate syrup and mustard are awesome, so I'd bet maple syrup and hot sauce would be pretty good, too."

"I'll take your word for it."

"My folks told me they'll be on the bus for eight hours. That would drive me crazy. I know! We should build a rocket ship."

"What are you talking about?"

"If we had a rocket, we could get places real fast. Like in the movie we watched yesterday. That was awesome."

"It wasn't awesome. It was crazy." We'd stayed up late Saturday watching *Super Danger Guys*. I'd wanted to rent something with fake dinosaurs, but Mookie was dying to see that one. "In real life, the kid would have just gotten hurt."

"Not me," Mookie said. "I'd go flying." He spun around and made *whooshing* sounds. The *whoosh* turned into a "Gaaaahhh!" when he tripped on his laces.

I guess he was right about going flying. But it was a short trip. The scream was followed by a crash as he tumbled into a couple garbage cans that were lined up at the end of a driveway. He knocked over one of the cans, spilling out a mess of leftover food, crumpled paper, and these large gray lumps that might once have been cat litter.

I went to help put the garbage back. That stuff doesn't bother me at all. I can look at the grossest pile of rotten half-eaten food without even feeling a quiver in my gut. Mookie had a pretty strong stomach, too. Once, he ate a pickle he'd coated with strawberry jelly and dipped in a crumbled fish stick, just to gross out a couple girls at another lunch table. But this stuff was making him gag. So I took care of most of the actual picking up while he stood next to me and made comments about the weirder and sloppier pieces.

"Whoa, that looks like a pig intestines."

"Ick—who'd throw away that much oatmeal?"

"Oh man, I think that's a diaper."

As Mookie was putting the lid back on the can, and I was wiping my hands in the grass, he said, "That's weird. I don't remember that bush."

"What bush?"

He pointed back the way we'd come. "By the blue house on the corner. That wasn't there before."

I looked where he pointed. There was a large bush right behind the last tree before the corner.

"So what. Maybe it's new," I said. "People are always planting things around here."

"I guess. But I hate when things change. It's hard to get used to new stuff."

We started walking again. But Mookie kept looking over his shoulder. "Ever feel like you're being followed?" he asked, a moment later.

"Only when you're behind me." Wherever we went, Mookie got distracted pretty easily. Walking with him usually meant I needed to do a lot of waiting up. Or backing up. And a bit of picking up, since this wasn't the first time in his life he'd collided with stuff. I figure he wipes out about five garbage cans on an average week.

"No. I mean secretly followed, like by someone who doesn't want you to know he's there." He turned around again. "Whoa!"

"What?" I really didn't want to get distracted. We were going to be late for school if he kept this up.

He grabbed my shoulder. "The bush moved."

"Knock it off."

"Really," Mookie said. "Seriously. I think it's following us."

"Bushes don't move."

"Right. And dead kids don't walk."

Okay, he had a point there. You could sort of call me dead. I didn't have a pulse or heartbeat. I didn't feel pain. I didn't need to breathe. But I could walk, talk, and think. Mookie liked to call me a zombie. I didn't totally agree with that, but I definitely couldn't explain how I was able to pass for a living kid. If I could walk, I guess a bush could move. I turned and looked.

"Whoa!"

The bush was still behind a tree, but it was behind a tree a block away from where it had been before. I stared at it, waiting to see if it would move again. But it just sat there, quivering slightly in the light breeze.

I didn't like mysteries. I walked toward the corner.

"What are you doing?" Mookie asked.

"Finding out what's going on," I said.

"Be careful, it might attack you. I've read all these books where people get killed in the African bush."

"I don't think it's the bushes that kill them. I think it's lions or something." I wasn't worried. It was a floppy-looking bush, with branches that drooped to the ground, and tiny green leaves. As I got closer, the bush started to inch backward, like it was trying to move without looking like it was moving. I dashed forward.

"Yipes!"

A man tumbled from behind the bush, landing on his butt on the sidewalk. The bush fell over and some dirt spilled out. It was in a large pot. I guess the man was trying to drag the bush and lost his grip.

That's really strange, I thought as I got a good look at him. He was wearing a green flannel shirt, green pants, green gloves, green shoes, and a green wool cap pulled low over his forehead—exactly what someone would wear if he was trying to blend in with a bush. He looked pretty tall, though it was hard to tell for sure since he was sprawled out on the ground. He had red hair, big ears, and a small birthmark on his right cheek shaped a little like California.

"Why are you following me?" I asked.

He stood up and dusted his pants off. "What an absurd question. I am not following you. Should I be following you?" He had an English accent, like the people in those infomercials who are trying to sound classy while they sell mops, vacuum cleaners, and grilled-cheese makers. "Is there anything that makes you followable? Are you expecting to be followed? Hmmmm?"

"No . . ."

"Well, there you go. I certainly wouldn't be following you, then. Would I?"

"Why are you dressed in green?"

"I'm Irish."

"You sound British."

"And you sound childish." He leaned over, reached through the branches, and grabbed the pot. "If you must pry, I am taking my new plant home."

I knew most of the people who lived along this street. Even if I didn't know all of their names, I knew what they looked like. I didn't recognize this guy. But I wasn't going to waste any more time thinking about it. There was no reason not to believe him. He could have just moved in. I'd actually be a lot happier believing he wasn't following me. The last thing I wanted was attention.

"Okay. Sorry I made you fall."

"I didn't fall. I have excellent reflexes. I was merely resting."

"Whatever." I trotted back to Mookie. "He's taking his new plant home. And he has excellent reflexes."

"This town is getting weirder and weirder," Mookie said.

My Rotten Life: Nathan Abercrombie, Accidental Zombie
By David Lubar

> ABOUT THIS GUIDE: The information, activities, and discussion questions that follow are intended to enhance your reading of My Rotten Life. Please feel free to adapt these materials to suit your needs and interests.

WRITING AND RESEARCH ACTIVITIES

I. Hurt-Be-Gone

1. Nathan hopes that the Hurt-Be-Gone potion will keep him from feeling blue. Imagine you could develop an amazing formula. What problem would the formula fix? What ingredients might you put in the formula? Find a large, clean, empty bottle or jar to use as a container for your formula. Make a front label with the formula's name and the problem(s) it should cure. Make a back label listing the ingredients, instructions for taking the formula, side effects, and other details you would like to include.

2. Make two "top ten" style lists: Great Reasons to Be a Zombie and Challenges of Being a Zombie. Copy one or both lists onto a large sheet of paper and decorate the margins with drawings, magazine clippings, or other art materials.

3. Instead of feeling no emotional pain, the Hurt-Be-Gone kills Nathan's ability to feel physical pain. Write a short essay describing what life would be like if you could feel no physical pain. What activities would become more dangerous? What risks might you take that you would not have taken before? Would you miss being able to feel pain? Conclude your essay with a recommendation to readers as to whether they should consider living a life without pain and why.

II. School and Home

1. In the character of Nathan, write an e-mail to your mom, dad, Mr. Lomux, or Mr. Dorian confiding what happened to you in Uncle Zardo's lab and your current "almost dead" status. Write a second, reply e-mail in the character to whom Nathan has written, sharing your reaction and advising Nathan on how he should handle the situation. If desired, write a third e-mail (or role-play a conversation) in which Nathan tells his friends about confiding in an adult.

2. Details like Nathan's mom's dead plants and Abigail's cluttered family car reveal the interesting home lives of characters in *My Rotten Life*. Informed by details from the novel and your imagination, draw a picture of one of the story's home-related settings using colored pencils, chalk, or pastels.

3. Nathan does not have a hand-held game device, such as a DS, nor does he have his own computer. Create a class survey about family technology and related rules. Include questions about how many computers are in the house, what gadgets kids own (cell phones, game consoles like X-Box or Wii, etc.), and what sort of rules about the Internet and e-mail are enforced in their homes. Compile the results of your survey in a chart or table to present to classmates or friends during a short summary presentation. Include your thoughts on whether Nathan's technology situation is similar to or different from that of most kids you surveyed.

4. How does Nathan reattach his snapped-off thumb? Use this information to write step-by-step instructions for young zombies on how to reattach broken body parts using household products. Individually, or in small groups, prepare instructions for what zombie kids should do if they have to eat food, how to remove forks or other utensils from one's head, or other critical young zombie tasks. Compile your instruction sheets into a handbook of advice for young zombies.

III. Creepy Classics

1. The author peppers his story with references to classic horror stories and films. Go to the library or online to learn more about one of the following names from the story: Belgosi (Béla Lugosi, actor), Dorian (*The Picture of Dorian Gray* by Oscar Wilde), Otranto (*The Castle of Otranto* by Horace Walpole), Romero (George A. Romero, scary movie director), Moreau (*The Island of Dr. Moreau* by H. G. Wells). Learn about the lives of the authors or directors, the stories in which these words are featured, and any movies, additional books, or other creative uses to which these names have been put. Compile your research on an informative, illustrated poster to present to friends or classmates. Discuss whether what you have learned about the names David Lubar uses in his book deepens your understanding or appreciation of the story and, if so, how.

2. Make a list of your favorite scary story titles, characters, authors, and movies. Then, select some of these names and words to use in an outline for your own three-to-six-page scary story. Your selected terms can be used to name people, animals, schools, streets, buildings, food brands, or any other story components you choose. Share your completed story with friends or classmates.

3. Uncle Zardo is a mysterious figure in the novel. Write your own "Biography of Uncle Zardo." Or, in the character of a television news reporter, prepare a short news report entitled "Uncle Zardo Sighted Again."

4. Create a new book jacket design for My Rotten Life or another favorite scary story. Include a front cover illustration with the book title and author's name and a design for the back cover, with a short, tantalizing description of the story below the heading "A Creepy New Classic."

QUESTIONS FOR DISCUSSION

1. How does Nathan describe the social seating in his school cafeteria? How do his descriptions help you to understand Nathan's personality? How do his descriptions compare to the way you might describe your own school cafeteria?

2. As My Rotten Life begins, Nathan uses physical terms, such as a ripped-out-heart and a screwdriver-stabbed tongue, to explore emotional injuries. Have you ever had your feelings hurt so badly it felt like a wound? What language would you use to describe such an experience?

3. Why doesn't Nathan have a PSP, DS, or other portable game toy? Why is this important? Is ownership of technical gadgets, such as game devices and cell phones, important at your school? Does being good at computer games matter? Why or why not?

4. On page 33, Nathan observes that "the whole world had done its best to take my breath away." How is this foreshadowing? What other images prepare readers for Nathan's zombie transformation?

5. Do you think Nathan means it when he wishes that he "didn't have any feelings at all"? Would you want to remove all painful emotions

from your life and, if yes, would you risk being a lab experiment to do so? Explain your answer.

6. In the chapters following the lab accident, what changes begin to happen to Nathan? How do these changes affect his routines and attitudes? How do Nathan's parents and teachers react to the changes?

7. What is Mookie's reaction to Nathan's being "dead"? How is Mookie a good friend to Nathan?

8. Why does Abigail hide her intelligence at school? Do you agree with her reasons for doing so? Why or why not?

9. On what adventures do Nathan, Abigail, and Mookie embark to find elements of the cure? What surprising things do the friends learn about one another in the course of these adventures?

10. How does being a zombie improve school life for Nathan? How does he react to his unusual athletic ability and resulting popularity?

11. Why does Nathan agree to go to Shawna's party after all? What happens when he arrives at the party with Abigail and Mookie?

12. How does Nathan's newfound understanding of the social scene help him get the charm from Shawna's wrist? How does his plan affect the social status of others at the party?

13. What does Nathan do when Abigail tells him that she could have made the cure without the last ingredients? How do you think you would have reacted? How does the cure work?

14. What events change the course of Nathan's cure? If you had been in Nathan's situation, would you have made the same choices? What is Nathan's zombie status at the end of the novel?

15. Abigail tells Nathan that ". . . a solution isn't like a piece of clothing. You can't always find one that fits the way you want." Give at least two examples from the story where this advice applies. Do you think this expression offers a good way to look at problems in life? Why or why not?